RIDING OUT THE TEMPEST

The Story of a Wounded Horse Healer

The Jack Harper Trilogy

Book 2

HILARY WALKER

Riding Out the Tempest

The Story of a Wounded Horse Healer

By Hilary C.T. Walker

* * *

Disclaimer

For My Son

Contents

A Few Words before We Begin ix

Chapter One: The Conversation 11

Chapter Two: The Bullied Kid 13

Chapter Three: Robert 18

Chapter Four: Jill Arrives 25

Chapter Five: Dinner but No Movie 36

Chapter Six: The Shelter 42

Chapter Seven: The Truth 55

Chapter Eight: Beckett 63

Chapter Nine: Church and a Fight 69

Chapter Ten: Father Michael............................74

Chapter Eleven: A New Home for 'Flex 82

Chapter Twelve: Joe's Return 88

Chapter Thirteen: Mrs. Ross 98

Chapter Fourteen: Down at the Cabin 105

Chapter Fifteen: Two Phone Calls 118

Chapter Sixteen: Joseph Harper 125

Chapter Seventeen: More Visitors 130

Chapter Eighteen: The Anguish 142

Chapter Nineteen: Hunting Dogs 145

Chapter Twenty: Departure Time Draws Near...153

Chapter Twenty-One: Revelations 156

Chapter Twenty-Two: Farewell 159

Excerpt from *Riding Out the Rough* 163

About the Author 175

Acknowledgements..176

Discover Other Books by Hilary Walker 177

Connect with Me..179

A Few Words before We Begin

The horse scenes in this book are all taken from my own experiences, although Jack is much smarter at dealing with difficult equines than I am!

The dog episodes are based on my son's dealings with shelter canines, one of which he ended up adopting. He is also a great dog trainer and I have copied his techniques throughout the trilogies.

The incident in the *Hunting Dogs* chapter closely follows what happened to my own dog.

*

In the foreword to *Riding Out the Devil* I mentioned how the idea for this trilogy came from my son's battle with ulcerative colitis, a devastating autoimmune disease.

Unless you know how to manage it.

UC sufferers do *not* have to let their lives be ruined by it.

My son's determination and success in overcoming his symptoms compelled me to create a fictional hero who has done the same. As I wrote in the first part of this trilogy: the world is ready for a hero with ulcerative colitis!

Enter Jack Harper, who leads a normal, active life thanks to following the natural diet from a protocol which doesn't resort to medication. All the food which Jack eats in the story is in line with the real-life treatment which my son follows. You can find the details of the disease and his diet at the back of *Riding Out the Devil* and for updated diet details please check my blog at *ChristianTales.com*.

If you or someone you know suffers from ulcerative colitis or Crohn's disease or any other form of IBD, *please* check out that information.

And now I hope you enjoy the continuing story of Jack Harper, the horse healer.

God bless,

Hilary

Rubesca4@gmail.com

Chapter One: The Conversation

Jack asked the mare to pick up canter.

Her tongue lolling to the left, she threw up her head and lurched into the gait with short choppy steps.

Jockey-style, he rose out of the saddle and invited the little chestnut to open up under him. She responded by lengthening her stride and settled into a smooth rhythm around the large outdoor arena.

Her name was Rustica and she was a skinny four-year-old off the racetrack. Jack took pains to explain to her owner that the ideal program for the Thoroughbred comprised short sessions of work, ideally on alternate days.

Consistent, correct riding would develop her muscles and fill out her body: sympathetic handling and plenty of turn out with other horses would calm her down.

Her many irritating habits would also disappear.

"But what about that tongue?" Mrs. Payne was an impatient woman. "How are you going to stop it from hanging out?"

"By ignoring it."

"What? How's *that* going to help?"

"Just wait and see," was Jack's answer.

Mrs. Payne scowled, but the trainer remained firm. "Well, I guess you know what you're doing."

"I guess I do." He gave her a disarming smile.

Rustica's right lead canter was unbalanced and awkward. She preferred galloping in the counter-clockwise direction of most American racecourses and Jack had to ask three times for strike off to the right before she obliged. After a full circuit of the arena he came down to a walk and scratched her withers as a reward.

He spent the next ten minutes cooling her off on a long rein and pondering his ex-girlfriend's enigmatic words over the phone at 1:30 a.m. yesterday.

Calling Jill in the U.K. was Jack's penance from Father Michael, given during Jack's unanticipated first confession in nearly two decades. He'd visited the priest over an entirely different matter and left as a reinstated, forgiven Catholic.

Jack's father and then the priest had clarified the cruel nature of his treatment of Jill. And so he had called to tell her how sorry he was for abandoning her seventeen years ago and demanding she terminate her pregnancy with their son.

His plan was to organize a memorial service for Baby Joe – as he'd named him. It would be held in his native England and he fervently hoped she would agree to attend.

But Jill's reply was unexpected.

"There's a lot more to it, Jack," she said. "We need to talk – in person."

"We can do that at the memorial service."

"No, we urgently need to talk *before* you organize it."

"Why?" he blurted out. He wanted to make reparation as soon as possible.

"It's a bit tricky."

Jack sighed. *This is why I work with horses! They're straight forward and don't over-complicate things.*

He then recalled that penance wasn't supposed to be easy. Taking a deep breath, he quipped, "O.K. Your place or mine?"

Jill laughed: she lived in the U.K. and would love to visit Jack at his Maryland farm in the U.S. She would call as soon as she had made the travel arrangements.

Jack breathed a private sigh of relief. He'd just spent a lot of money on that recent trip back to England for his mother's funeral, not to mention time he could ill afford to be away from his training business.

He heard from Jill later that day, giving only her flight details and revealing nothing further.

Now he spent every spare moment wondering: *What was the 'lot more to it'?*

Chapter Two: The Bullied Kid

Jack felt Rustica's taut body slowly unwind as she lowered her neck and stretched it out, snorting happily.

He patted her softly: she was a good horse and he was pleased with her progress.

Looking forward to a well-earned lunch, he dismounted and led the mare out of the arena as a familiar dark blue sedan drove past and parked outside the farm house.

Katie, the Golden Retriever, shot over to the battered vehicle, barking a loud welcome.

Jack groaned. He'd forgotten about the arrival today of the bullied boy Father Michael wanted him to help.

Her tail wagging furiously, the dog circled the priest as he exited his vehicle, while Jack forced his mouth into a welcoming smile.

The pastor bent down to pat Katie, his voice annoyingly cheerful. "Hello, girl, how're you doing?" He straightened up and waved. "Jack! I come bearing someone who'll be of tremendous use to you." He leaned into the car and said to his passenger, "Come on out! Mr. Harper is looking forward to meeting you."

I never said that! Jack thought, watching a thin sixteen-year-old climb out.

With a start, he recognized him as the boy he'd given his card to when the teenager was being bullied by taller team mates in town.

A tingle went down his spine. Here, surely, was Divine Providence at work: witnessing that incident had caused Jack to agree to help 'some kid' the priest was asking him to take under his wing. Father Michael had said he didn't believe in coincidences…

Jack led Rustica over and shook his hand. "Hi, Robert, good to see you again."

"Hello, sir," Robert took the proffered hand, eyeing the chestnut with anxiety.

Katie rushed over to the youngster, who fell on his knees in the dust with open arms. The thrilled dog piled into him and licked his face. Robert laughed. "Hey, hello, girl!"

Jack was ready to pull her off, but there was no need. This boy was a dog lover.

Katie adored young people and she was missing Joe, the teenager who recently brought his horse to Jack for help. The two of them had formed a strong bond, and she'd been moping ever since Joe's departure.

She was definitely taking a shine to Robert.

"Do you have a dog?" Jack asked.

Robert stood up. "No, sir. I'd love one, but my dad is allergic to pet hair."

Katie leaned into his left leg and, being fairly short for his age, the boy didn't have to lean over far to ruffle her ears.

"Well, it looks as if you have one while you're on this farm. Katie will be following you everywhere."

Robert beamed. "That's fine by me!"

The Retriever looked up at him with worshiping eyes and he squatted down again to rub her chest.

While the dog had the kid's attention, Father Michael took Jack to one side. "When Robert heard we were coming over to your place, he told me how you gave him your card after a bullying incident in town." He grinned. "This was meant to be, don't you think?"

Jack nodded and rolled his eyes. Was his life ever going to be under his control again, or would his mother be in cahoots with God and this priest until the day he died?

The barn manager walked out of the stable building and took the mare's reins from his boss.

Jack introduced him. "Luca is my right-hand man, and a very important member of my staff. You'll have a lot to do with him as well as me."

Jack liked the way Robert immediately extended his hand to Luca. It showed not only good manners, but also that he wasn't intimidated by people who treated him with courtesy. He would fit in very well.

"Welcome aboard, Robert." Luca gave him a big grin, and led the mare away to her stall while Jack invited his guests to join him for lunch.

"I warn you, my diet is enormously healthy. It may not suit you, but *I* have to stick to it so I make all my visitors do the same. I only have food in the house that I can eat."

Robert looked puzzled.

Jack looked at Father Michael, who said, "I thought it best if you told him."

"Father is referring to the fact that I have ulcerative colitis. It's an autoimmune disease affecting my digestive system."

"Sir?" Robert was even more confused.

Jack continued, "If I eat the wrong foods they trigger a reaction in my body, which attacks its own cells. I control the disease with correct diet and supplements."

It still amazed Jack that he was able to talk openly about this embarrassing condition, which for so many years he'd been desperate to keep secret. Meeting Joe and helping him overcome his own ulcerative colitis had changed that.

"That sounds painful."

"It is if I don't eat properly. So forgive the rather unusual and limited menu." He ushered them into the kitchen. "Meet another vital member of my staff. This is Luca's mother, Felicia, chef and housekeeper extraordinaire. Felicia, this is Robert."

The matronly woman wiped her hands on her apron and surprised the teenager with a hug. "Welcome, welcome!" she cried in her unmistakable Mexican accent. "Hello, Father!" she added.

"Don't I get a hug, too?" the priest complained, walking towards her.

"Holy men no need hugs," she announced, backing away from him. "Seet down, seet down! I bring food!"

Jack was grateful to her for not complaining about the unannounced extra mouths to feed.

*

Father Michael said grace, and Jack noticed that Robert went through the motions of joining in, but without conviction. The priest appeared not to notice.

Over the meal Jack explained his daily routine of riding the horses with Luca and his other rider, Frank, and performing stable chores. Robert would be involved in the handling of the horses on the ground as well as feeding, watering and cleaning stalls.

He observed, "You seemed a little wary of the horse I was holding just now."

"I've never been around a horse before, sir. It was kinda big."

Jack laughed. "Actually, she's a very *little* mare. You'll see some bigger horses later on. But you'll get used to them," he added encouragingly. "Those fellows who were pestering you in town are nothing in comparison. And horses respect leadership from their humans – just as bullies respect those who stand up to them. Working here you'll learn some useful tips for dealing with people who try to shove you around."

"That would be great, Mr. Harper. I want to learn everything I can."

Father Michael smiled at him approvingly.

Jack said, "'Mr. Jack' will do nicely, Robert."

After lunch he accompanied the priest to his car.

Predictably, the ever-zealous cleric used this opportunity to give the trainer another task. "Jack, technically Robert's parents are parishioners. But they don't go to Mass regularly, so their son's faith is weak, to say the least. This would be a good chance for you to share yours."

Jack grimaced. "I've only just come back into the Catholic Church myself, Father! And don't forget – I still have some reservations. I'm not qualified to help Robert."

"You're exactly the right person, Jack. You came back to the Church despite your objections, and can point Robert in the right direction – including encouraging him to come to me about any questions you can't answer yet. And don't forget, I'm always available to discuss *your* issues with the faith, too." He opened his car door. "Just see what you can do for Robert whenever the occasion arises."

Jack's eyes narrowed. "It'll cost extra, Father – a lot extra." Robert's parents were happily paying for Jack to spend time building up their son's self-esteem, even though he would be working on the farm.

"You can't put a price on faith, Jack. Good-bye!"

That priest had an uncanny knack of wrangling things out of him. But how was a newbie like himself supposed to evangelize a kid?

He shook his head and walked back into the house.

Chapter Three: Robert

With Katie's help, Robert quickly settled into the farm routine. It was agreed that his mother would drop him off at 7:30 a.m. Monday through Friday, and pick him up at 4 p.m.

Jack eased him into working around horses by giving him tasks which didn't involve direct contact with them. He wanted to accustom the lad to their presence without his having to get close to them.

Frank and Luca showed him how to rinse out the water buckets in each stall and fill them with fresh water. He learned to make up feeds and give each horse the right hay quantity.

Throughout the day he helped clean stalls so they didn't need tidying after the horses were turned out in the evening.

Robert started each morning on those chores. During that time the three men brought in the horses, then joined him. If Jack and his staff performed the same menial tasks as the newcomer, Robert would – Jack hoped – feel part of a team instead of low man on the totem pole.

Luca and Frank would treat the boy with respect, and Robert was polite with them.

And, as predicted, Katie became the boy's shadow.

At the end of the day the four of them would sit in the barn aisle on assorted stools and tack trunks cleaning the saddles and bridles. Luca and Frank downed a cold beer while Jack and Robert drank bottles of cold water from the fridge in the tack room.

The July days were hot, and the team was glad to rest in the cross-breeze wafting through the central aisle to rehydrate before continuing their work.

With the contented Retriever lying next to him, Robert helped wipe down the bridles and wash off the bits without getting water on the bridle leather. He was shown how to dismantle a bridle and put it back together.

"We pull the bridles apart and clean them thoroughly once a week," Jack told him. "That way the leather stays supple and lasts longer."

He was taught how to apply special soap to the saddles, wash the saddle pads and get horse sweat off the girths. He swept the barn and learned how to roll exercise bandages the correct way. By the time Friday of Robert's first week rolled around, it was clear the boy's help was considerably speeding up completion of the day's chores. As a result he was running out of things to do while the three men rode and Jack was concerned that he would become bored.

Until he saw the kid using his spare time to teach Katie tricks.

The horse trainer was riding in the outdoor arena with Luca and Frank, trying to get their sessions in before the July heat became too much for man and beast alike, when he spotted Robert with the dog by the front doors of the barn.

Jack had never formally trained the animal. But when Robert motioned her to sit, she instantly obeyed and he gave her a reward. He asked her to lie down and Katie dropped to the ground.

"Good girl!" Robert said, giving her another treat. "Break!"

The dog jumped up and followed her new master into the barn.

Jack smiled. *So that's where the boy's real passion lies!*

A few days later, when Mrs. Riceman arrived to pick up her son, Jack saw Robert's disappointment. He was loath to part from Katie, lying next to him in the barn aisle. Reluctantly he rose from the tack trunk and the Retriever padded alongside him.

Jack said, "Hey, I see you've been working with Katie."

"Sorry, Mr. Jack. I sometimes have some time between chores. I hope you don't mind."

"Not at all. She's much better behaved now." On impulse he said, "I wonder, would you be willing to stick around an extra hour in the evenings to work with her?" More time with the dog every day would be a reward for his hard work.

Jack sensed his two staff members staring at him. Like their boss, they had no idea what Robert could teach Katie that would make her useful for farm life. It wasn't as if they needed her for cattle or sheep herding. What had got into the horse trainer?

No matter, Jack told himself, the point was to make Robert feel good about himself. Success in training Katie would be part of that process regardless of whether or not it benefitted Jack's business.

His mother's voice echoed in his head: *You don't need me anymore to help you act on your better instincts.*

Seeing Mrs. Riceman walking towards the barn, Robert hastily answered, "That would be *awesome*! I know tomorrow's Saturday, my day off, but could I come back just for a few hours? You know, to reinforce what I've taught her this week?"

Jack nodded. "Sure. If your mother doesn't mind, I've no objection."

Robert approached her with Katie on his heels. "Mom, can you bring me back tomorrow? Mr. Jack wants me to train his dog. I've already taught her some stuff. Watch."

The kid gave a demonstration. Katie perfectly executed the command to sit, lie down, and back away – a move which Jack hadn't yet seen her do.

He looked at Luca and Frank, who had come out to observe. "Now that *could* come in handy."

They gave him a sardonic smile. "Sure thing, boss," Luca said.

Jack's eyes narrowed.

Robert's mother said, "Great job!"

"So I can come back tomorrow?"

She wouldn't refuse her son, considering how his short time on the farm had already improved his outlook. She glanced at Jack, who gave the thumbs up and she beamed. "Are you *sure* you don't mind having Robert for an extra day, Mr. Harper?" To her son she said, "You make sure you help out before spending time with the dog, right?"

"Sure thing, Mom. Thank you, Mr. Jack and see you tomorrow, Katie!"

He told her to sit while he got into the Camry. The dog looked wistfully after the car as it drove away.

Jack whistled and she reluctantly returned with him and the two grinning men to the barn. He scowled: "Not a word from *either* of you!"

*

Watching Robert work with Katie that Saturday was a welcome distraction. Jill was scheduled to arrive tomorrow at 1:50 p.m. and her ex-boyfriend was becoming increasingly nervous about this reunion.

Before setting off for Dulles, Jack would attend his first Sunday Mass as a returned Catholic – and he wished these two highly emotional events weren't happening so close together. He strongly suspected that Someone Upstairs had arranged this on purpose.

'There are no such things as coincidences.'

But those were tomorrow's problems.

Today Jack was impressed with Robert. True to his word he diligently carried out barn duties before playing with Katie.

Saturdays were 'spa' days for certain horses. Most of them were ridden on the five weekdays but there were exceptions like Rustica. These animals were ridden on alternate days.

The more skittish ones, or those that were sore or sour, were given chiropractic treatment and/or massages on Saturdays, as Jack had no time for those during the week.

He invited Robert to watch him with the little ex-racehorse in her stall.

"I haven't finished making up evening feeds," he said.

"I know, but today's a slow day, and Luca is happy to pick up the slack for you."

The teenager stood obligingly in the aisle and observed Jack working with the mare.

"I bet you're wondering why I want you to see me do this.'

"Yes sir, to be honest, I am."

"Well, you're being so helpful with the chores around here that we're getting through them fast. And I know you want to work with Katie, but I was hoping to give you more confidence around the horses first."

Jack grinned at the boy, who looked poised to flee. "Don't worry, I'm not going to make you come in the stall this second. I just want you to see how calm horses can be, and how we can help them reach that state."

Robert leaned over the half-door looking more relaxed.

Within moments Jack could see he was mesmerized as the mare transformed under the trainer's hands.

Jack ran his fingertips along what he called the horse's bladder meridian, lightly running them over a line behind the mare's poll, a couple of inches down from the central line of her body.

"I'm following the method devised by Jim Masterson[1], in his book 'Beyond Massage,'[2]" Jack explained. "Watch for her to blink or yawn when I get to certain places. There she goes!"

As he touched her neck about a foot behind her poll, Rustica blinked. Jack kept his fingers on that spot while the mare gave a huge yawn, and at the same time her eyes appeared to roll back on themselves.

"She's releasing tension," Jack explained. "This little lady spent her early years cooped up in a stall. She had no opportunity to stretch her legs in the paddock and graze like a normal horse, the way she does here on the farm. As a result she's stored up a lot of stiffness in her body, and I'm encouraging her to let go and relax her muscles."

Robert observed Jack perform the same routine on the horse's other side, followed by some exercises to stretch her neck and release tension in the poll.

"Do you feel a little less scared of her, now?"

---

[1] To see demonstrations of how this is done watch Jim Masterson on YouTube: Masterson Method Bladder Meridian – Going into Detail

[2] Beyond Massage by Jim Masterson

"I guess," Robert said unconvincingly.

This kid is way more interested in dogs than horses, Jack thought. But if he could get Robert to come into the stall with him, it might help him stand up to bullies at school. Dealing with his fears of something physically stronger than him had to help. And because Robert was short for his age it made sense to start with this small horse.

"Try it," Jack said.

The youngster took a deep breath and came into the stall.

"Close the door – she won't squash us," Jack told him. "Hold your hand out so she can smell you. Don't be timid, or she'll think there's something to be worried about."

"That's like with dogs," Robert said. "You have to be calm around them and then they'll be calm around you."

"That's exactly right. There you go. Now take your left hand and run the tips of your fingers along her neck about four inches from her crest – that's where her mane is."

"Like this?"

"Just like that."

Under Jack's guidance, Robert performed the same techniques he'd watched the trainer do.

"See what a soft eye she has?"

Rustica suddenly shook her head and Robert leapt back.

Jack grinned and put his hand on the boy's shoulder. "That's a *good* thing, son. She's letting go of her tension. That's one of the ways a horse does it."

He watched Robert tilt his head to one side and examine the mare. "Now she looks kinda sleepy."

"Sure she does. She's super relaxed and standing quietly, with her head low and her ears in neutral."

"Just like a dog," Robert remarked again. "But why is she yawning like that?" He retreated again.

"Dogs yawn, too, don't they?"

"Yeah, they do, but it's not always a good sign."

"Here it *is* a good sign. She's still releasing tension."

"She sure is *very* tense."

"Yup, but it's great she's letting me help her unwind."

"She really trusts you, Mr. Jack."

"The secret is to behave as if I know what I'm doing. If I act with calm confidence around her, she'll respect me and be willing to let me be in charge. I bet Katie respects you because you exude quiet confidence and authority." Jack paused as Robert nodded thoughtfully then continued gently, "It's the same with people who try to push you around."

The kid looked at him. "Do you really think I can learn to stand up to them?"

"Look at how well you're doing with Rustica, and she's ten times their size!"

Robert grinned and Jack told him that next week he was going to help bring in the horses.

He was ready.

Chapter Four: Jill Arrives

Katie stared at her master, head tilted to one side while Jack knelt by his bed praying. The Retriever was still confused by her owner's new nightly routine.

Dear Lord,

Thank you for the good things that have happened today. Robert's doing well, with Katie's assistance (he gave the dog a quick stroke under the chin) *and I think he'll be able to stand up to those bullies by the time he leaves here. Thank You for using me to help him.*

But I'm going to need Your help to get through tomorrow!

I'm looking forward to receiving You at Mass in the morning, but after that, Lord, I don't know how things will go between Jill and me.

I'm really going to need Divine Assistance!

Thank you.

Amen.

He made the sign of the cross and got into bed, but couldn't sleep with the cacophony of thoughts competing for attention in his head.

This time tomorrow Jill would be here!

What did she look like, now? Was she the same Jill he knew at university?

Not being a fan of exposing his life to the world, his online presence was restricted to a business website. But he had discovered Jill on Facebook under her real name, Penny Sharpe.

Wishing to put the past behind him, he'd not wanted to look her up before. Now that she was about to step into his world again, he wanted to find out as much about present day Penny as he could.

There wasn't a whole lot to glean. She didn't post frequently, so her life was a mystery beyond the fact that her status was 'single,' she worked at a local bank in Somerset and had a lot of Facebook friends.

Several recently uploaded photos would prove helpful with identifying her tomorrow at the airport.

She was still recognizable. The long blond hair she'd sported at university looked more businesslike in its shorter style, and her naïve blue eyes were more somber. Jack suspected the responsibility for that rested squarely on his shoulders.

But what he really wanted to know he couldn't find out from the internet.

'There's a lot more to it....'

A lot more what? Had there been complications with the abortion? Did she have physical problems because of it? Had she subsequently tried to have children and was unable to, as Jack had read can happen in these instances?

Had she been married, and her husband divorced her because he wanted children? Had Penny been abandoned twice by the men in her life?

Or, on a happier note, did that mean his son had not been sacrificed to the selfish whims of the father?

Jack wanted so badly to believe that God had spared their child!

For the millionth time he prayed the latter was true, before falling asleep at 1 a.m., exhausted.

*

The next morning, Felicia said, "You still want Luca and me to come to your English Mass today, *si*?"

A few weeks ago, Jack had attended his mother's funeral Mass as a dedicated non-believer – little knowing he would soon be back in a Catholic church as a bona fide member of the congregation.

He felt rather foolish, a grown man wanting company at his first Mass in seventeen years as a practicing Catholic. But he swallowed his pride. Penny could come with him next Sunday and his staff would go back to their Spanish service.

"If that's still alright by you both, Felicia, I'd really appreciate it."

"We glad to come."

"I'll drive," Jack said.

He opened the front passenger door of his white Range Rover Evoque for Felicia, and her son Luca climbed into the back.

Pressing the engine starter, Jack thought back to the morning when Luca had driven his mother and Joe to church, six weeks ago. The kid had been so skinny that he fit perfectly into the narrow space between mother and son on the one and only seat of Luca's well-worn pick-up truck...

How was Joe doing? Hopefully he was managing his ulcerative colitis symptoms and enjoying a successful show season with his horse, Duke. The kid deserved it: he'd had a raw deal with his father dying, and then his diagnosis, followed by the accident with Duke that had wrecked their relationship for a long while and brought them both to Jack's farm.

He would love to hear from the teenager and know that all was well with him.

Our Lady of Sorrows Church came into view. The lot was filling up, so he dropped Felicia and Luca at the front of the building and found a space to park.

He walked towards the beautiful stone building with its tall tower and bells pealing a loud invitation to worship. He admired the statue of Our Lady as he passed it on his way to the open doors of the church.

Underneath the life sized Madonna a plaque read, "Our Lady of Sorrows, pray for me."

How had Jack missed the fact that the church his parents attended back home in England – and where his mother's funeral took place – had the same name as this, his new Mass venue?

A frisson pulsed through his body.

He had not yet been inside the actual church building, having only visited Father Michael's office in the administrative wing. He smiled, recollecting that day when he'd parked as far away from the holy edifice as possible to avoid being mistaken for a practicing Catholic.

The priest had made short shrift of him: here he was, voluntarily walking into Mass. Life was strange indeed!

Luca was waiting outside the church with his mother, and the three of them walked in together.

*

Jill's flight (she'd always be Jill to him) was expected on time at 1:50 p.m.

Felicia and Luca celebrated Jack's first Mass by having breakfast with their boss after the service before he left for Dulles.

He could have done without their company during the meal: his mind was churning and he wanted to think in peace. But coming back to the faith *was* a big deal and he appreciated their kindness in being with him at church this morning as he received Communion for the first time in over seventeen years.

Now breakfast was over and it was time to drive to the airport. While he was gone Brad would see to everything. An older man who worked at the racecourse in a former life, he helped with Jack's horses on Sundays when the staff had the day off.

Yesterday Jack had taken his Evoque through the car wash and vacuumed out the interior. He realized how superficial this was – trying to let Jill see how well he was doing – but the activity had also been a welcome distraction.

The hour and a half trip to Dulles afforded Jack the time he craved to mull over the morning's events.

One of the attractions of the Catholic Mass is that wherever you are, the liturgy is the same. Although in the vernacular of each country, the ritual is identical the world over.

It amused Jack that this sameness was the very thing he'd hated as a child and teenager. The tedious predictability of it all, the never changing format.

Yet today he'd *enjoyed* the fact that the service was indistinguishable from the Mass he'd attended in England for his mother's funeral. Both churches being called Our Lady of Sorrows had strengthened his sense of belonging.

During the exchange of the sign of peace, Jack was pleased to have two acquaintances with him. He wouldn't have to shake hands only with total strangers.

He was standing at the end of the pew by the central aisle, preparing to extend his hand to the parishioners behind him, when Father Michael grasped his new recruit with both hands in a hearty shake.

"Welcome back, Jack! Peace be with you!"

Jack was dumbfounded, for the priest had walked halfway down the aisle to greet him. He pressed the pastor's hands warmly. "And with you!"

Then – oh, joy! – unlike that awful funeral when he was the villain who'd let his mother down because he wasn't in a state of grace – this time he'd been able to receive Communion!

I hope this makes up for it, Mum!

He sensed her presence beside him as he took the Host and drank the Precious Blood from the chalice.

After Mass Father Michael was standing outside the church greeting everyone as they left. He said a few words in Spanish to Felicia and Luca which Jack didn't understand, then said: "Good to see you, Jack! Robert's behaving himself, I hope?"

"He's a good worker, Father. And before you ask, no, I haven't evangelized him yet."

The clergyman gave a broad grin. "All in good time! I have faith in you."

As the three of them walked across the parking lot to the Range Rover Jack felt sorry for people who don't understand the joys of believing in a good and bountiful God. He guessed it was why Father Michael had the irrepressible need to spread the Good News far and wide through any means possible. And he clearly considered Jack to be one of those means.

Oh, well, all in good time …

*

Jack arrived in Dulles with thirty minutes to spare and stood awkwardly in the International Arrivals Building. He wished he'd brought a copy of Jill's photo with him for reference then remembered he could pull up her Facebook page on his cell phone.

After ten minutes of checking her photo against the emerging passengers, even though it was far too early for her to be here, he decided to find a gift store. A few minutes later he returned to his post bearing a box of chocolates and a Hermès scarf.

It was rather unlikely that this gesture of goodwill would help break the ice after seventeen years, but it was better than standing with empty hands.

A new group of suitcase-dragging passengers came through the doors. Jack scrutinized the labels on their luggage and saw Jill's flight number on them.

A slim woman emerged and his heart beat faster. She was Jill's height, with shoulder length blond hair and blue eyes, scanning the crowd of greeters. Their eyes met briefly, but she continued her search and her smile settled on someone else.

Would he recognize Jill from those Facebook photos? Would she recognize him? Hopefully she'd checked his website. Had he changed a lot over the years? So concerned with whether she was the same, he'd not even thought about how different *he* might look now.

He began to worry that she might be disappointed in his appearance.

I wish this were over!

He felt idiotic, standing there with his chocolates and expensive gift and suddenly thought with horror, *What if she construes them as a romantic gesture?*

Women could be so funny – they tended to read more into everything than a man.

Should he ditch them, just in case she misunderstood his intentions? Now he wished he hadn't bought them – but on the other hand, he'd have felt a real cad if he'd not got her *something* ....

"Jack, is that you?"

Obsessing on the stupid gifts, he'd stopped looking out for her. And here she was, standing right in front of him after seventeen years.

Her desk job at the bank hadn't done her figure any favors: there was more of her now than when they were at university. But not everyone could earn a living being physically active.

Jack told himself not to be judgmental and stood uncomfortably as these thoughts ran through his head.

Her blond hair – a different shade from his memories of it – was drawn back and held by a large tortoiseshell clasp. The rather official hairdo, together with the beige slacks, plain yellow cardigan and flat tan shoes suited her career as a bank teller.

Jill laughed and the action softened the hard look of her blue eyes. She pointed at Jack's gifts. "Are those for me?"

"What? Oh, yeah!" He stuck out his hands in a graceless gesture.

"How about a hug first?" She stretched out her arms.

Jack responded by clumsily placing the chocolates round her left shoulder and the scarf round her right. If only he hadn't bought them!

Her perfume had a slightly citric quality to it. "It's great to see you," he said, releasing her. "How was your flight?"

"Not too bad. There was a little turbulence when we took off from Heathrow but it eased off. The meals were good, as they usually are with British Airways. And I got to sleep a bit."

"That always helps on long-haul flights," Jack responded, offering his gifts again.

He observed her take them, as if watching a bizarre movie in which his two disparate worlds were merging. He couldn't decide whether it was a good thing or not.

"Oh, you shouldn't have," Jill laughed self-consciously at the cliché.

Jack grinned. "Probably not, but have them anyway."

"How many horses did you have to ride to afford this scarf? It's gorgeous!"

"So you *have* been checking on my line of work."

Jill looked askance at him. "I got your phone number off your web site, silly."

"Makes sense." He wasn't keen on being called 'silly.' Were they already that familiar again? He didn't think so. But perhaps he was being oversensitive. "This way to the parking lot." He took her large and heavy suitcase, glad of the rollers: it was a long walk to his vehicle.

When Jill saw the Evoque she whistled. "I'm impressed, Jack. Nice wheels!"

Jack had cleaned it on purpose to elicit this response. Yet, oddly, he didn't like her reaction – there was something vulgar about it.

You're being very critical for a chap who went to his first Mass this morning, Jack! What happened to removing the beam in your own eye, first?

He felt ashamed of himself and opened the passenger door for his guest. "I'm glad you like it."

With her suitcase safely stowed in the back of the vehicle, Jack got in and switched on the engine. Once more, Jill was in awe.

"Don't you need a key?"

"Nope. As long as my key is physically in the vehicle, all I have to do is depress the brake pedal and push the start button."

"I still drive an old-fashioned manual car."

The engine purred as Jack negotiated the multi-story garage and paid at the exit.

"What do you have?"

With sadness he noted how this conversation mirrored the stilted one with his father two months ago. Did they have nothing to say to each other beyond banalities? Was the whole of her visit going to be like this?

"Well, I obviously don't earn as much as you do. I have a Jeep Patriot. It's got a lot of miles on it, but it's reliable."

"That's a good vehicle," Jack remarked. "Did you need all that room for a particular reason?" He was really fishing for subjects.

"Yes, it's for Molly, my Old English Sheepdog. Even with the rear seats lying flat, she takes up the whole of the back!"

"That's a fun breed. What do you do with her while you're at work?"

"I go home at lunch time and let her out."

"You must live very near your job." *Oh, this is awful!*

"I do, and the bank closes promptly so we get to go home on time every day."

"Do you work on Saturdays?"

"We have a rotation: I have to go in once a month. What about you? How many days a week do you work?"

And so it went, lurching from one superficial topic to another, all the way back to the farm, without Jill alluding once to their baby. She clearly didn't want to talk about him yet, and Jack realized he would have to be very patient and wait until she was ready. It was going to be a long hour and a half.

He dutifully answered her questions about the horses he had in training, how many acres he had, and the number of people who worked for him.

The closest she got to anything personal was to mention his ulcerative colitis.

"How are you getting on these days? Do you still have your symptoms under control?"

"Yes, thankfully." He longed to tell her about Joe, and how he'd been able to help the kid get his life back. But for some reason he didn't feel she would be interested and it made him feel further away from her than ever.

"So," he continued, "I'm afraid it means you're stuck with my diet."

"That's fine," she said, "I remember those days, and they weren't that awful."

"My housekeeper Felicia is a genius for creating tasty dishes with the limited list of food items I can eat. I think – and hope – you'll like them."

Jill reached her hand across the central console and squeezed his knee. "I'm sure I will, Jack, don't worry."

Not ready to return the gesture, he gave her a strained smile and said, "That's great."

Her brief show of affection reminded him of one piece of information he needed to give her before they reached the farm. It would have a strong bearing on their relationship throughout her stay.

"Jill, are you still a practicing Catholic?"

"What a silly question, Jack! After everything that religion did to our relationship? Of course not! Why do you even bring it up?"

He took a deep breath, sent up a quick prayer to God and his mother, too. This would not go well.

"I felt that way for a long time, too. In fact, it sounds as if I left the church at the same time you did."

"I sense a 'but' coming on." Jill sounded wary.

"I haven't told you yet, but my mother died last month."

"Oh, I am sorry, Jack."

"Thank you. I flew back for her funeral and after I came home, well – a whole lot of things happened to me in a very short space of time. I came back into the Catholic Church the day before I called you."

Jack was unprepared for Jill's reaction. She clapped her hands and burst out laughing. "Oh, Jack, you always were the jokester!"

He gripped the steering wheel as an intense anger rose in him.

Stay calm, Jack, stay calm!

Mum! Help me! Holy Spirit, where are you?

She was making a mockery of possibly the most important event in his life and dismissing his dearly held experience of having been forgiven.

He suddenly needed Father Michael. He would sort Jill out, without lashing out at her, as Jack so longed to do!

She was still laughing when they reached the electronic gates to the driveway.

While they were opening, Jack turned to Jill. "I'm deadly serious. I went to my first Mass this morning. I hope that during your stay I'll be able to convince you to return to the faith as well."

Well aware of the practical implications of his statement, as had been his intention, she retorted, "Well, Jack, if you hadn't treated me the way you did, I wouldn't have left the church in the first place."

Touché!

Chapter Five: Dinner but No Movie

The lush green paddocks on either side of the drive leading up to the farm house moved Jill to say, "This is *beautiful*, Jack!"

Grateful for the change in subject, Jack replied, "Welcome to my humble abode."

"But where are the horses?"

"They're in their stalls. During the summer we turn them out at night. It's too hot for them in the day and the flies really bother them."

"Do you have only clients' horses here?"

"Mostly. A few are mine."

"Do you really ride *every* day?"

"Pretty much. Saturday is an easy day and my barn staff has off on Sundays, as do the horses."

In the center of the circular drive in front of the house stood a fountain with a large rearing horse that spewed out water into the surrounding pond.

Jack parked the Range Rover and Jill got out to admire the rambling, single-story brick house and long white porch.

She could see the large barn building off to the left. A few inquisitive horses were poking their heads through the stall windows which opened to the outside.

"If I'd known how you lived, I'd have come over a long time ago!"

I don't think so! I refused to talk to you for seventeen years, remember?

"Only the house was here originally and it needed a lot of renovation. The land was cleared, but I put in the barn and the fencing plus the riding arena and the indoor arena."

"How long has it been finished?"

"It became fully functional about ten years ago." He took her case out of the vehicle. "Come on in, I'll show you around."

He gave her a tour of the house and showed her the room where she was going to sleep. Then he asked if she wanted to see the barn?

"My Sunday help is there, and I need to help him feed the horses before turning them out and cleaning their stalls."

"Don't you ever get a day off?"

"Nope!"

"Then I'll get a shower and pass on the barn tour. I can catch up with you when you get back from your chores."

Jack felt a guilty relief. He was already longing for some space – without her in it.

He greeted Brad in the safe haven of the barn. Although aware his boss was picking someone up from the airport today, the ex-racing man knew better than to ask questions. The two slid into their tasks as if Jack had been there all day.

Being around the horses was far easier than dealing with the complicated emotions of a woman who held resentment towards him and mocked his religion.

By contrast, he appreciated the friendly whinnies of his equine guests as they anticipated feeding time, and their snorts of contentment while they munched on hay during the wait for dinner.

The stalls were already clean and Jack was annoyed there wasn't much left to do. The sooner the barn chores were finished, the sooner he'd have to go back into the house…

This past week he'd not given much thought to their sleeping arrangements, beyond having Felicia prepare a spare bedroom for Jill. But his ex-girlfriend's derision of Catholicism on the very day of his first Mass was too much. He couldn't handle the thought of their sleeping under the same roof and desperately needed to be alone.

Felicia had left a great meal for them in the fridge. Thankfully it would only need reheating and not a long preparation time.

The two men sprayed the horses with fly repellent and turned them out for the night. The stalls were immaculate, the feeds made up for the morning, and there was nothing more for him or Brad to do. With a heavy heart Jack thanked his helper and walked back to the house with Katie.

The dog had given Jill a very lukewarm reception. Normally she showed wild enthusiasm for every visitor, regardless of gender.

She'd followed Jill and him into the house and politely accompanied them on the tour of the place, but had chosen to trot behind Jack to the barn instead of spending time with the newcomer as was her habit.

That had to be significant, he thought, patting the Retriever on the head.

When Jack entered the kitchen, Jill had changed clothes and he didn't care for the overly short skirt.

He was glad Robert wasn't around, and made a mental note to tell her there was an impressionable kid on the premises during the day and she'd need to dress more modestly. Although he had no idea how to achieve that without upsetting her, given his experience of her so far.

"Hi!" he said as cheerily as he could. "Good shower?"

"Oh, yes!"

"Can I offer you something to drink? Wine, perhaps?"

"I could use a large glass of red."

She walked towards him but Katie placed herself between them. Though surprised, he longed to say 'Good girl!'

He laughed and said lamely, "Katie is used to having me all to herself."

Normally you don't care. What's up, girl?

He reached for a bottle of red wine from the rack built into the kitchen island and busied himself with opening it. Katie stuck very close to him.

After handing Jill a full glass, he took their dinner out of the fridge. Felicia had put the food in dishes that would look presentable on the table after he'd microwaved their contents.

Jill was ready for her second glass of red wine by the time dinner was ready. He gave her a refill and poured himself a gluten-free beer.

His ex-girlfriend picked up her knife and fork.

Though fearing another fight, Jack stopped her. "I say grace before meals now, Jill." He made the sign of the cross. "In the name of the Father and of the Son and ..."

"Oh, for heavens sake, Jack! Spare me this farce!"

"... of the Holy Spirit, Amen."

"This is ridiculous! I'm going to start eating!"

Jack ignored her. "For what we are about to receive, may the Lord make us truly thankful. Amen." He crossed himself again. "In the name of the Father and of the Son and of the Holy Spirit. Amen."

As he began eating his food, he had the vile sensation that the Devil had just invaded his home.

Trying to ignore that uncomfortable episode, he did his level best to keep the talk on benign issues throughout the meal. But it cost him great effort and he couldn't wait for the evening to be over.

She kept leaning uncomfortably close across the kitchen table and emptying her glass faster than Jack felt was good for her.

How was he going to survive a whole week of this?

By the end of dinner, through judicious questioning, Jack had at least gleaned that she'd been in several relationships since Jack's departure seventeen years ago, had never married and was currently 'single' in the Facebook sense of not having a boyfriend.

Although Jack had been away from the dating scene for a long time, he picked up on Jill's cues: she was clearly hoping to rekindle their romance.

He had never felt further away from her than he did now and it would be despicable of him to play along just to retrieve the information he wanted. Yet he was desperate to find out what had happened to their baby.

Maybe his father was right: perhaps she simply needed to feel that he cared about what had happened to her? Taking a deep breath, he looked into the blue eyes staring disagreeably close into his, and reached across the table to take one of her hands.

"Jill, I know I caused you a lot of pain and I want you to know I'm very sorry." He squeezed her fingers for emphasis.

Tears started to dribble down her cheeks and she nodded, very slowly.

"It was wrong of me, terribly wrong, and I regret my actions. You need to know that."

There: he'd said his piece and now she should accept his apology and tell him what she'd meant by 'there's a lot more to it.'

She seemed to expect more. But what else was there to say? And why was she closing her eyes like that and leaning even closer towards him?

With sudden revulsion he understood. *Oh no! She's expecting me to kiss her!*

Jack was caught between a rock and a hard place. If he kissed her, she'd get the wrong idea. If he didn't, she'd get mad and never tell him anything. He was wondering how long he could leave her suspended like that, when Katie barked loudly. Thankful for her intervention, he sprang up from the table.

The front door had been left ajar. Tigger, the ginger and white barn cat, had sneaked into the kitchen from outside and the Retriever was preparing to give chase.

Jack swiftly picked up the cat and carried him out into the evening. He deposited the purring animal on the porch table underneath the nascent moon and rubbed his back for a moment.

Things were getting crazy. But he couldn't stay out here all night – he had to get back to the kitchen and deal with the situation in there.

It had taken care of itself. Her long flight, combined with imbibing too much wine and leaning forwards so far towards him with her eyes closed, had resulted in her head landing on the table. By the time Jack returned to his guest, she was sleeping peacefully in that position.

This now presented a problem of a different nature. Should he take her to her bed or leave her there? He decided the gentlemanly thing was to carry her into her room and lay her on the bed.

But on awaking the next morning, she'd wonder what she was doing lying on a strange bed in her clothes. He wrote her a note and left it on the bedside table.

He then packed clothes and toiletries into his backpack, locked the door of the farm house and drove with Katie to the cabin by the lake.

Chapter Six: The Shelter

Jack watched the sun rise through the cabin windows the next morning and remembered why he was here.

With a groan he got out of bed, showered and dressed, then drove back with Katie to the house.

Jill wasn't yet up. Felicia was in the kitchen making coffee for her and setting out Jack's usual breakfast fare of blueberry and strawberry yogurts, chocolate chip bread and coconut milk.

On the stovetop was a fry up of zucchini, gluten-free pasta and green peppers in olive oil, sprinkled with salt and pepper and the anti-inflammatory ginger and turmeric powders.

"'Morning, Felicia."

"Good morning, Señor. You think your guest eat your food?"

With any luck Jill had meant what she said about being happy to eat Jack's bizarre diet. "She has no choice."

Sincerely hoping his house keeper would stick around and thereby reduce any awkwardness, he fed Katie and sat down to eat. He had things to do and couldn't wait for Jill to appear.

Felicia said, "I leave coffee pot on and come back later to clean house."

"Thank you."

Twenty minutes later Katie scooted out onto the porch at the familiar sound of the Camry and Jack followed. Jill would surely know to find him at the barn.

Mrs. Riceman waved at Jack from her car and drove off, leaving her son for the day.

Katie bounded over to Robert, who said, "Sit!" and she instantly obeyed, tail wagging. "Good girl!"

Jack smiled: the kid and that dog really loved each other.

The three of them walked to the barn where Jack was glad to be back in his daily routine and pretending that Jill wasn't in the house.

Remembering his words to Robert about helping to bring in the horses this week, he demonstrated how to lead a horse on the animal's left side, with the right hand holding the rope a couple of feet below the horse's chin and the other end with his left hand.

He said, "Don't ever loop the rope around your hand or fingers. If the horse were to suddenly pull back, you could break your wrist or even worse. I have a friend who lost the tip of his thumb from carelessness like that." He showed the correct way with the horse he was leading. "And like I told you on Saturday, stay relaxed and the horse will, too."

Katie stuck like glue to the youngster, whom she hadn't seen for a whole twenty-four hours, as he checked today's schedule on the bulletin board outside the tack room. He noted the first rides of the morning and carried their tack over to the saddle racks and bridle hooks outside their stalls.

While the horses digested their food and the men sat together discussing the training plan, Robert taught Katie to fetch, using an old sponge that Frank had thrown away.

Watching the boy, a plan formed in Jack's head. *I must remember to bring it up at lunchtime.*

The men split up to make the lunch feeds and distribute hay, giving the horses more time to digest their breakfast before being groomed and saddled.

This was Robert's cue to stop playing with Katie. Frank had volunteered to teach him how to groom the quieter horses and tack them up.

With Frank helping Robert, it would take longer to get through all the horses today, but would save time in the long run. For Robert would be able to get the animals ready for all three of them once he became comfortable with his new duties.

Jack's first ride was Goliath, the big flea-bitten gray. For two weeks the sour show-jumper had been taken on trail rides, away from the arena. He'd enjoyed walks through the woods behind Jack's farm, and canters around the fence perimeters in addition to very light flatwork in the outdoor and indoor rings. But no jumping.

Today Jack was reintroducing the gelding to the idea of negotiating poles in the outdoor arena.

He'd set up an innocuous line of three trotting poles on the ground plus another set of six poles. One pole lay separate from the others for the horse to walk over a few times first.

Initially the horse high-stepped the single pole until he realized Jack was only asking him to walk over it in a long frame on a loose rein.

Once Goliath was comfortable doing that, Jack urged him into a trot over the same pole before riding him towards the row of three.

Even with Jack's light seat and soft rein, the horse tensed up at the sight. He launched himself at them, clearing the trio of poles in one leap. Afterwards he bucked and cantered around the arena for a lap.

Jack rode out this predictable reaction and gradually brought Goliath to a halt. "Let's try that at a walk now, shall we, buddy?"

The distances were incorrect for walk, but the animal needed to go through a few times slowly and learn to negotiate one pole at a time.

Initially, Goliath's large hooves hit the poles, which upset him. It took a few minutes for him to settle so Jack could ride him quietly over all three, with the horse adjusting his stride so as not to touch them.

The gelding became excited again when he faced the same line at a trot. Jack turned him onto a circle until he could maintain a steady rhythm.

This time the horse approached the line calmly. He still raised his feet with exaggerated energy, as if expecting the poles to scorch him, but Jack praised him for his effort.

It took several more goes, in both directions, before the jumper realized that nothing difficult was being asked of him.

Finally, Jack was able to trot him through the line of six poles on a long rein. The horse lowered his head and relaxed into this easy job.

He brought Goliath down to a walk and scratched his withers. "Good work, old boy."

He became aware of a female figure leaning over the arena fence. Wondering who it was and why she was there, he suddenly recalled that he had a guest – and not any guest. *Drat! Jill! I forgot all about her!*

With a forced smile he rode over. "Good morning! How did you sleep?"

"Very well, thanks." She lowered her voice. "I didn't do anything stupid last night, did I?"

"No, why?" Jack said innocently.

"Oh, no reason. So this is what you do all day?"

"This is how I earn a living, yes. I wish I didn't have to ride while you're here," he said untruthfully, "but I have to keep my clients happy, otherwise they won't pay me."

What a turnaround from a few days ago when he'd wished he could take the time off to spend with her!

"I'm almost done with this guy, so if you don't mind waiting a while longer?"

"Not at all! I'll admire you from here."

Jack walked the horse around the arena for five minutes before dismounting. Jill walked with him and Goliath to the barn, where Robert was holding Rolando, his boss's next horse.

Katie pressed in closer to her new friend as Jill approached, a fact which couldn't have escaped Robert, either.

"Good for you, Robert!" He grinned at the teenager, standing so boldly next to the black Thoroughbred. "Thanks for tacking him up for me." He turned to his ex-girlfriend. "This is Jill – I mean Penny," Jack said, shaking his head at his mistake.

Jill laughed. "Jack used to call me Jill when we were at university together," she explained. "But my real name is Penny."

Robert had taken Goliath from Jack and was handing over Rolando's reins. Unable to shake her hand, Robert nodded to her. "Hello, Ms. Penny. Glad to meet you. You're from England, too?"

"Yes. Jack and I go back a long way." She grinned at the trainer in a way that made him uncomfortable.

He gave an awkward smile.

Lucas was now heading towards the barn with the horse he'd been riding in the indoor arena. Jack was anxious to keep on schedule. "Thanks, Robert. Your next horse is coming in. I'll get out of your way."

"Sure thing, Mr. Jack. See you, ma'am." The youngster led Goliath away, with Frank along to help. Jill accompanied Jack back out.

The whole morning was like this, with her watching him, following him back into the barn and back out again as Jack rode three more horses. Used to working by himself, he hated this close scrutiny.

At the same time he felt guilty. What else was she supposed to do? She had no interest in horses, and was here to see him. *That* she was doing for sure!

Lunchtime came around and Jack was grateful for Robert's presence at the table. It would postpone any tricky conversations and was also an opportunity for him to put his new idea to Robert.

They sat down to a meal of chicken breasts fried in olive oil, gluten free polenta and boiled cauliflower with carrots. Felicia had also prepared a salad of lettuce and baby spinach leaves with olive oil and balsamic vinegar, salt and pepper. To drink there was iced spring water.

Jack closed his eyes and said grace aloud. This time Jill waited patiently for him to finish before starting to eat.

"You did a great job with the horses today, Robert," Jack said. "It hasn't taken you long to become more confident with them."

"Thanks! I guess the more time I spend with them the less frightening they'll be."

"Yup!" Jack turned to Jill. "You should have seen Robert backing away from a really small horse I was holding when he first got here, only last week. He's a quick learner."

Jill added, "I notice that you get on well with Katie, too."

"Yeah, she's a great dog! I'd love to have my own dog, but my dad's allergic to them."

"Which brings me to an idea of mine, Robert, which I think might interest you."

The youngster stopped eating as Jack continued. "The dog shelter in town is always looking for volunteers to walk the dogs. They're stuck in cages for 24 hours a day. The place needs help from someone like you, who understands dogs. What do you think?"

Robert's eyes opened wide. Then his face fell. "But I'm supposed to be here all day. That was our agreement."

"You're soon going to be helping so much that we'll get through our work in double quick time."

Jack reasoned that his job was to give Robert self-confidence. Since the kid's real passion was dogs, not horses, why not let him spend time with canines, too? And it could save his parents some money, since they wouldn't have to pay him for Robert's time at the shelter.

"We could easily spare you for, say, a couple of mornings a week. If your parents agreed to drop you off at the shelter first thing, I could pick you up at midday and bring you back here for afternoon chores. What do you say?"

"That would be *awesome*!"

He felt Jill's approval from across the table. "I only have two more horses to ride after lunch, which gives us time to go and check out the shelter. Why don't you call your parents and see what they think of the idea?"

Robert left the room, Katie in tow, and Jill remarked, "That was a kind thing to suggest, Jack."

"Yeah. He likes dogs a lot more than horses, that's for sure."

Robert came back five minutes later, looking happy.

"I take it they're O.K. with the idea?"

The teenager nodded vigorously.

Jack said, "Well, I'd better ride those two horses so we can go into town afterwards. Come on, Robert, I need your help."

Jill shadowed him until his afternoon's training was done. Robert helped prepare feeds with more alacrity than usual, and the horses were turned out by 4 p.m.

Jack reassured him, "Don't worry, Robert, I called the shelter and they're open till 6. We have plenty of time to make it before they close."

At 4:15 p.m. the three of them set off.

The shelter was on the outskirts of town. The big square building was one story, and furious barking could be heard as soon as the Evoque turned into the parking lot. A girl with the tattoo of a ferocious looking bulldog on her neck was exiting with a large German Shepherd on a leash. Excited to be out of his cage, he was dragging her down the sidewalk.

Robert observed, "She's going about it all the wrong way."

Jack and Jill looked at each other, bemused.

"What *should* she be doing?" Jack asked.

"For a start, the collar should be higher up the dog's neck so she's not pulling on his throat and damaging it. She'd also have much more control that way. She needs a slip leash."

"Sounds as if you *are* just the kind of person this place needs!" Jill said.

"Here's hoping!"

Jack parked the vehicle and Robert fairly ran to the entrance. He opened the door for Jack and Jill to pass through.

Inside, the barks were deafening. Jack could distinguish different types and pitches of noise coming from the inmates. Some of them sounded aggressive, others were whining and still others howling. It was distressing: serving an undeserved prison sentence, they were desperate for release.

Jack walked up to the lady behind the desk, who looked at him hopefully. "Have you come to adopt?"

"Not to adopt. But this young man is brilliant with dogs and interested in volunteering."

Robert stepped forward and gave her a charming smile. "Yes, ma'am. I would love to walk your dogs for you."

Although this wasn't her first choice of answer, the lady was still pleased to have a potential dog walker on her hands. However, she looked skeptically at the short teenager. "Do you have any prior experience?" she asked.

"Er – no," he stuttered.

"How old are you?"

"Sixteen," he said stoutly.

"He's done a great job with my dog," Jack added.

"How about letting me show you that I can walk your dogs?" Robert suggested.

"Well," the lady said, "it's not as if we have too many walkers." She paused. "O.K. then." She looked at Jack. "I take it you're his dad?"

Why do people always think I'm a father?

"Nope, but he works for me and his parents have agreed to let him volunteer here. His mother will be dropping him off here, so she can sign anything else you need her to."

"That'll do. Follow me, then." Jill walked behind Robert and Jack as the lady led them through a swing door and into the canine cacophony.

Jack couldn't remember seeing such a sad sight. Some dogs rushed to the front mesh of their small areas, wagging their tails and hoping to be noticed. Others cowered at the back, hoping not to be noticed. Still others sat hopelessly on their beds, as if ready to give up on life.

Jill voiced what the three of them were feeling. "Oh, it makes you want to adopt them all!"

"It does, doesn't it?" Jack admitted.

"Is this a kill shelter?" Robert asked anxiously. He was standing in front of a sad black dog with a few white points. The label on the mesh read, *Beckett.* "I've read that black dogs get chosen last and don't always make it that long…"

"We don't believe in putting dogs down just because they've not been adopted."

Robert looked relieved. "Could I take this one for a walk?"

"You're welcome to try. But he's not interested in anything or anyone and we've had a hard time persuading him to come out of there."

"What happened?" Jack asked.

"Oh, he's done nothing wrong. But his owner died three weeks ago, and he doesn't want to eat, either."

"The poor thing!" Jill exclaimed.

"Do you still want to try and coax him out?" the lady asked Robert.

"Yes, ma'am!"

"I'll get his leash then." She walked over to a panel on the wall covered in hooks holding different leashes, and picked out a stout blue one. "Here you are." She fished in her pocket and pulled out some treats. "These might help."

Robert took them and the leash from her as she opened the cage door. "Do you mind shutting me in with him?"

Surprised, the lady said, "Sure."

The three adults looked on with curiosity as Robert walked onto the concrete floor and sat quietly in the corner by the door, facing Beckett, but not looking at him.

He threw a treat on the floor close to the dog. The animal flinched at the motion and retreated further into himself. But Robert waited. He still didn't make eye contact with the animal and pretended to be interested in the dog next door.

Once Beckett was sure of not being watched, he stretched out his neck to smell the treat, eyes never leaving this new human in the corner of his cage. After a couple of minutes he relaxed enough to snatch it up.

Robert moved nearer and placed another treat by Beckett's bed, still looking away from the dog. It only took a few seconds for the animal to grab this second tidbit.

Without standing up completely straight, so as not to intimidate him, Robert quietly but confidently moved towards the dog's bed and sat by the edge, with a treat on the palm of his hand and still not making eye contact.

Jack could see Robert breath deliberately slowly, just as he himself did with a nervous horse. In fact, the whole process was uncannily similar to his own techniques.

Slowly Beckett stretched out his neck again, his nose twitching as he smelled the food. Robert continued to sit still as a mouse, but Jack saw his eyes look towards the dog.

Ever so softly, still anxiously observing the youngster, the dog placed his muzzle on Robert's hand. He then stole the treat and took it back to his bed.

As the dog chewed on his prize, Robert moved onto the bed with him. Beckett's eyes registered this change in the human's position, but he continued to chew.

"There's a good boy," Robert said encouragingly, and laid his hand on Beckett's back. The black dog stopped chewing and turned his head around to see what the boy was doing. Robert gently massaged the length of the animal's spine and Jack could see the dog visibly relax under the boy's hand. Beckett calmly returned to his treat.

The kennel lady whispered: "That kid really does have a knack with dogs. Beckett hasn't let anyone touch him since he came in two weeks ago!"

"Robert is taking the time to show the dog he can trust him." Jack knew the importance of this from his dealings with horses. So often, owners moved too quickly around their equines and scared them. Then they became annoyed at the animals' subsequent nervousness, caused by the owners themselves.

The kennel lady sighed. "I wish we had time to do that with all the dogs. It just shows you how badly we need volunteers who do have the time and patience – and the know-how to help them."

"I imagine you're very busy," Jack said, and she nodded wistfully.

Still sitting next to the dog, Robert was now affixing the leash to his collar. He let go of it and stood up. Turning away from Beckett, he walked towards the cage exit without a word.

For a moment the dog lay in place, watching the teenager leave. Then he rose from his bed and padded behind. Jack could tell Robert was aware of this, but acting as if he weren't.

The teenager waited by the mesh door, facing the adults.

Beckett came alongside and sat down next to him, looking up at this human with new hope in his eyes.

Robert inclined his head towards the black face with the white muzzle and smiled. "Hi, Beckett. Want to go for a walk?"

The dog seemed to understand and began panting with excitement. Robert picked up the leash and said to the astounded kennel lady, "We're ready to go now."

The walk went well. Jack and Jill sat outside on a bench and watched Robert take the happy animal down the road. Beckett started out pulling on the leash, but Robert placed the collar higher up his neck and corrected him a few times. The dog obeyed by heeling properly which his previous owner had clearly taught him to do.

By the time the two of them turned down a side road, Jack felt they were a good match and he needn't worry about them. The kid might be his responsibility, but he needed time alone with the animal.

"That was a smart suggestion," Jill said, as soon as he was out of earshot.

"What was?" Jack asked.

"Putting forward the idea that a bullied kid like Robert take shelter dogs for walks. Exerting authority over them will definitely raise his self-esteem."

"Yup! That's the idea."

"You're a good man, Jack Harper."

Unsure where this was heading, he gave an enigmatic smile – designed to satisfy her without inviting further comment.

It didn't work.

"Perhaps we'll have some time alone this evening to talk?"

Jack was dreading a tête à tête with Jill, yet how else was he going to find out what had happened all those years ago?

Without enthusiasm, he said, "Sure. Let's talk over dinner after Robert goes home."

Jill patted his hand, which annoyed him. "Great! I look forward to it."

Robert reappeared with Beckett walking sedately beside him. The teenager was over the moon, as was the kennel lady, who'd come out to check on the duo.

With his mother's prior permission, Jack signed as Robert's guardian and her son was all set to walk dogs at the shelter on Tuesday and Friday mornings while he was out of school. Mrs. Riceman would drop him off in the a.m. and Jack would pick him up at midday and bring him back to perform his farm chores.

All the way back he was singing Beckett's praises. "He's such a cool dog. It's real sad his owner died."

"How lucky you came along to keep him company until he finds a forever home," Jack said warily.

"I just wish Dad weren't allergic," was Robert's predictable response.

"But you've taught Beckett that he can trust another human." Jack was determined to keep the kid's thoughts firmly on the idea of a future home elsewhere for the black canine.

"Yeah, I guess."

"You can do that for all the other dogs, Robert, and make it easier for them to get adopted, too. You'll be doing them a great service. Beckett isn't the only dog that needs a new home."

"I guess," came the half-hearted reply from the back seat.

"For sure!" Jack said with conviction.

Shortly after their return to the farm Robert's mom arrived to take her son home. Jack told her how well the trip to the shelter had gone, adding to a very animated account from the dog walker himself.

He was annoyed when Jill joined them – then felt guilty. What else was she meant to do? She'd been at the shelter with them, too.

Listening to her son, Robert's mom looked at Jack as if to say 'What have we started?'

He smiled at her. "He's got a real talent with dogs, and they *respect* him."

She nodded in understanding. Her bullied son's self-esteem would grow as much from being around dogs that listened to him as from spending time with adults who treated him fairly.

A happy Robert ruffled Katie's ears and got into the car. "'Bye, Mr. Jack. 'Bye, Ms. Penny. See you tomorrow!"

As they drove off, Jack realized he hadn't introduced Jill to Robert's mother.

Chapter Seven: The Truth

He decided against explaining himself.

"O.K." he said as brightly as he could, "I'll go back to the cabin and get a shower. Then we can sit down together and have a drink before an early dinner. How does that sound?"

"What's up with your going back to the cabin?" she snapped.

Jack replied, honestly, "It looks better if a single guy and a single woman aren't sleeping under the same roof, that's all."

"You *have* gone all religious, Jack!"

"I don't want anyone on the farm to feel uncomfortable. My staff is Catholic as well as me, and we need to be respectful of them."

And you should respect my wishes, too!

Before she could make a retort, he said, "I'll be back in an hour. C'mon, Katie!" He knew the dog would follow him anyway.

Jack and the Retriever piled into his old pick-up. In his rear-view mirror he could see Jill watching him leave, her arms angrily akimbo.

*

An hour later they were both sitting on the front porch. Jack had given Jill a very large glass of red wine to save frequent refills and opened a gluten-free beer for himself. Katie lay on his feet, and from afar they looked like a regular couple enjoying a drink together.

Jill had changed into a white summer dress. She must have bought it for this trip, as he could see little occasion for her to wear it in England. In her hair she'd placed a clip decorated with a flower. Definitely not your average British outfit.

Jack was in jeans and a light blue shirt. He'd exchanged his paddock boots for soft moccasins, which he found comfortable after a day's riding.

To keep the atmosphere light, he clinked his beer bottle against Jill's glass.

"Here's to old friends catching up!"

She responded with, "Here's to not-so-old friends catching up!"

Felicia appeared on the porch. "Mr. Jack, you want I bring dinner out here?"

"That's a great idea. Jill?"

She gave the housekeeper a brilliant smile. "I'd love that. Thank you!"

Felicia nodded and disappeared back into the house.

Jack and Jill looked out over the circular drive and listened to the soothing tones of water cascading from the rearing horse into the fountain pool.

Beyond, the driveway extended several hundred yards down to the electronic gates. The horses had been turned out for the night into the paddocks on either side and were grazing contentedly, swishing their tails against the flies. Every so often one would turn its head around to swat a bug off its flanks.

Tigger broke the tranquility by jumping onto the porch. He marched across with his tail raised vertically in a deliberate attempt to rile Katie. She took the bait and sat up, ears forward and alert, ready to give chase.

Remembering Robert's training methods Jack said, "Leave, Katie!"

She looked up at him hoping he didn't mean it.

Robert said that a command should only be given once.

That hadn't immediately made sense to Jack, but then Robert showed him the clip where Cesar Millan poses an interesting question to a retired police officer who's having problems with his dog.

If the ex-lawman were to approach a suspect and say, 'I'm arresting you – no, seriously, I'm arresting you. I mean it. I really do!' would he have the person's respect? Would he be obeyed?

The answer was, of course, 'no.'

Once, said with authority, should be enough to get the desired result. If not, moving towards the dog makes him feel uncomfortable and encourages him to do the right thing.

Again, Jack could relate this thinking to his horse training. He shouldn't be surprised: horses and dogs are both pack animals in need of a strong leader.

Katie was still staring fixedly at Tigger, so Jack tapped her on the back to get her attention. She glanced at him dolefully and lay down while her eyes followed the annoying feline as he paraded down to the other end of the long porch. With a backwards glance at the dog, he jumped off and trotted over to the barn.

"Good man, Tigger. Go catch some mice, will you?"

"Do you get mice here?" Jill said nervously.

"Oh, sure. Mice, rats, raccoons, possums, snakes, poisonous spiders, groundhogs, skunks – you name it, we have it."

"That's a vicious line up! Sorry I asked!"

"They usually venture out at night. Tigger comes in useful, but he doesn't normally go for the larger, dangerous animals." Jack grinned. "Although he has turned up in the morning with the odd scratch on him. I think he sometimes takes on more than he should."

Felicia came out carrying a tray.

Jill jumped up. "Let me help you." The two of them arranged the food and glasses of iced water on the long wicker table. The house keeper had also brought out the opened bottle of red wine which she placed near Jack so he could top up his guest's drink.

"This all looks wonderful!" Jill gushed.

Felicia looked meaningfully at Jack. Was she trying to convey that he ought to say the same thing more often? Or that he should pursue a relationship with Jill?

He flashed her a brilliant smile, which she was welcome to interpret anyway she liked.

"I go now, Mr. Jack. Dessert is in fridge."

"Thank you, Felicia. Have a good evening."

He and Jill were alone: time to get the answers to some burning questions.

He took a last sip of his beer. Mindful of his father's words to him, after Jack admitted abandoning Jill to abort their baby, he asked as gently as he could, "Did anyone go with you to the clinic that day?"

He glanced sideways at her and her expression hardened.

"No," she whispered hoarsely. "No, they didn't."

"Did anyone else know?"

"No." She bit hard into a piece of broccoli.

O.K. fine. It was natural she get her own back on him by making him do all the work. This must be part of his penance. Chewing on a forkful of minced beef and carrot, he wondered what to say next.

He cleared his throat. "Were you able to say goodbye? Was he a boy, as you thought?"

Jill's blue eyes were pure ice. "Yes, I *was* able to say goodbye to *your* son."

Jack swallowed hard, imagining how awful that must have been. What a total bastard he was to leave her to deal with this on her own!

'You do realize that's murder son, don't you?' his father had said.

Jack sat numbly, not knowing what the appropriate reaction would be. Then he sensed the quiet presence of his deceased mother.

Remember, Jack, God has already forgiven you, even if Jill hasn't.

He so needed to hear those words! Jill being here had taken the bloom off the excitement of going to his first Mass and Father Michael's warm public greeting. This confrontation with an aggressive non-believer was tough to handle.

This is so hard, Mum!

Again, her serene words soothed him.

You're not responsible for how she takes your apology.

However, he was still facing an irate woman, wondering how to make her feel better.

What do I say that will help?

The answer was immediate.

Ask the Holy Spirit to give you the right words.

Of course! Jack hadn't prayed at all before starting this conversation!

Thanks, Mum!

Slowly he sipped on iced water while offering up a prayer request as his mother had suggested. Jill's frostiness made it hard to talk to her, but he must if he wanted answers – and to give her the closure his father said women need.

"Jill, over the phone you said 'there was a lot more to it.' What did you mean?"

She was still evasive. "I was surprised to hear from you, and it was early in the morning."

"Yes, I'm sorry about that."

"I was pleased that you did, though." Her tone sounded conciliatory: that was a good start.

"It came out of the blue, I know," Jack admitted.

"What prompted it?"

Jack was loath to give her the real reason, given her anti-Catholic stance. He gave the short version. "My mother's death."

"Jack, again, I'm so sorry! You should have said something!"

"It was hardly appropriate." He paused, "But actually very relevant to my calling you."

"Oh? How so?"

Jack told her about flying over for Mrs. Harper's funeral and confessing to his father that he had got Jill pregnant and deserted her to have an abortion alone.

Jill was staring at the wooden planks on the porch. "What was his reaction?"

"Being a staunch Catholic, he made it very clear to me that abortion is murder and that I was in a state of mortal sin by making you do it. He pointed out that the baby wasn't just yours – he was ours, and that I had killed our son."

"But how did *that* prompt you to call me?"

"Well, like you, I left the Church after we separated. It's a long story, but a series of events led to my seeing the local parish priest."

"Is that when you became Catholic again?"

"Yes."

"So, it's only very recent?"

"Yes. It was the day before I called you."

"That is recent! Tell me all about it."

Jack was more than willing to explain his story. But not now, when he was so close to getting the answers he wanted from her!

"Sure! But first, please tell me what else happened the day you went to the clinic for the – er – " His voice trailed off.

At the time he wanted Jill to get rid of the baby, he'd had no problem saying the word 'abortion.' But now, back in the Church and fully appreciating the horror of what he'd put Jill and the baby through, he was unable to say it aloud.

"Jack," her voice was softer, "do you ever wonder what our son would look like today?"

"Yes," he replied miserably. "I do."

"Well, I don't know whether either of us will ever know. But I needed to tell you this face to face: I didn't go through with the abortion."

Jack was stunned. Was she saying that his son wasn't dead?

He suddenly became angry. He'd been beating himself up for so long over something he hadn't actually caused. But, he quickly reminded himself, he had fully *intended* it to be done, which was just as bad.

His ire switched to jubilation. "So, our son is still alive?"

"As far as I know, yes."

"'As far as you know'? What do you mean?"

"Jack, I wasn't ready to have a baby any more than you were. But I was still Catholic enough in those days to believe that abortion was wrong, and when I saw my little boy in that sonogram sucking his thumb ..."

Jack suddenly felt jealous that Jill had seen their son performing that innocent act.

If you'd stayed with her, you <u>would</u> have seen it.

"Oh, Jill, I should have been there."

"Yes." She was staring at the porch floorboards again.

"So, what happened to baby Joe?"

"Joe?" Her voice sounded vacant.

"Yes. Remember? When I called you, I said that I call him baby Joe, after my father." One day he would tell her the other reason he'd chosen that name.

"I'd forgotten." Her voice trailed off. She appeared captivated by the fountain fixture and was no longer concentrating on their conversation.

"Did you keep him?" Jack prodded.

"No."

This was infuriating!

"But you said he was alive, as far as you know." He wanted to shake her. Why didn't she come out with it?

She looked at him, her blue eyes misty. "Yes, I hope he is."

"Well, obviously so do I. But what happened?"

"A really lovely couple adopted him."

Jack took a few moments to take this in. He'd just learned that his son had not been aborted. And now he was to understand that the boy belonged to other parents. His heart was beating fast and his palms began to sweat.

Dear God, this is hard!

Yet did he even deserve to know that Joe was still alive, after what he'd done to Jill?

A little voice said: *You thought you had blood on your hands and should thank God that you don't.*

Through wanting to expiate for the murder of his baby, he'd discovered that he actually hadn't killed him. And if his penance from Father Michael hadn't been to phone Jill and apologize to her, he'd never have known the true fate of his child.

God works in mysterious ways!

Jack told himself to be grateful for this knowledge.

It's not your will be done, Jack, but God's.

Anticipating his next question, Jill said, "No, I don't know who the parents are. I didn't want to. It was better that way, otherwise I might have tried to interfere in his life later, when I was on my feet financially."

Jack's heart sank at this. "Is there no way to find out?"

"Even if we could – and I don't think we can – would it be fair on him if we were to suddenly intrude on his life? And it's not as if we're a married couple. Having each birth parent living on a different continent would just add confusion to his life. I don't even know whether his adoptive parents have let him know he's adopted."

Jill had obviously thought long and hard about this over the intervening years.

He couldn't fault her logic. She was right: it would be upsetting for their son to suddenly be confronted with an extra set of parents, who weren't even together.

That could be of no possible benefit to the teenager and Jack must be satisfied with the knowledge that his baby boy was not aborted and thank God for it.

And there was someone else he needed to thank. "Jill, it was very courageous of you to continue with the pregnancy after I left. It means a great deal to me to know that my son didn't die because of a bad decision of mine."

"My then Catholic conscience gets all the credit. There was enough of it left to save our son, at least."

"About that – "

"No, Jack, it's too late for me to go back now. I've left the Church and that's that."

"Once a Cath – "

Jill raised her hand. "Nope."

Chapter Eight: Beckett

Robert phoned later that evening. The lady at the dog shelter had called to ask him back the next day, Wednesday, even though his normal days would be Tuesday and Friday.

"Her regular person called in sick, but the dogs still need exercising," he told Jack, who hated to let his efficient helper go. But the teenager wasn't here for Jack's benefit – it was supposed to be the other way round. And it had been *his* idea in the first place for the youngster to work at the shelter.

When Jack picked Robert up at noon the next day, the kid was full of enthusiasm for his new job.

"Did you walk Beckett again?"

"Uh-huh! He's *such* a neat dog once you get to know him."

Just how well could you get to know a dog so fast? Jack wondered wryly. "Did it take you long to get him out of his cage this time?"

"That's the amazing thing. He immediately recognized me and ran to the front. And we had a long walk."

"What other dogs did you take out?" the trainer asked, concerned about where this volunteering gig might lead.

"There was a cute Jack Russell who wanted to pull all the time, so I let him out in a little grass pen they have and played with him before I took him for a walk. He was good after he'd got all the extra energy out of him.

"Then there was a Golden Retriever, a little Katie. She's awful young, and they told me she'd been tied up to a tree by the road. A driver saw her and took her to the shelter. People can be so cruel. Why do they do that to an innocent animal?"

"I don't understand it either, son. But let's be glad she was brought to a safe place, and hope she finds a good home soon."

Robert continued to chat about the dogs all the way back, with Beckett featuring more prominently than the others.

Perhaps he should let the kid work full-time at the shelter?

"You know, you don't have to come to my farm anymore if you don't want to."

"Aren't you happy with my work, Mr. Jack?"

"I'm *very* happy with your work! I really missed you this morning. It took twice as long to get through the horses. But your real interest is helping dogs, and you should pursue your passion. That's what I did."

"Yeah, I do love being around them. But I also like being around you guys. I wanna keep helping you, if that's O.K."

"Works for me, Robert. Then we'll stick to your Tuesday and Friday routine at the shelter, shall we?"

As they approached the house, Jack could see Jill helping Felicia set out their lunch on the porch table. The weather had been comfortably warm over the past few days and the large overhead fans discouraged flies as well as improving airflow.

"I'm starving!" was Robert's greeting to Felicia and Jill.

"Then sit down and eat!" Felicia said, with a grin.

She hovered over the boy, pouring him a large glass of coconut milk with cocoa powder and coconut sugar in it.

Jack smiled. The kid was used to this food now – and so was Jill. Having ulcerative colitis meant that Jack couldn't afford to take any chances with his diet. He had to stay healthy in order to train horses and earn a living, so his guests had to eat what he ate. It was that simple.

Of course, Jill already knew that. At university in England when they were close, she had been wonderful about adjusting her eating habits to be in tune with his. He'd always been able to count on her for that.

So why were they so out of sync now?

She was different. There was a new edge to her. One minute she wanted to rekindle their romance then the next take him on a guilt trip.

I suppose it is my fault.

But guilt was not a good basis for a relationship. He couldn't see the two of them getting back together now, any more than he'd been ready to marry her when she became pregnant.

The situation was tricky and he couldn't see a happy resolution.

Over lunch Robert said to Jack, "Could you pick me up a little earlier from the shelter tomorrow?"

"Sure. Why?"

"Well, it's just that I'd really like you to watch me with Beckett. I take him out last."

Where was this going? Jack wondered again. *As if I can't guess.* He tried to sound upbeat. "How does 11:30 sound?"

Robert beamed. "Awesome!"

"Perhaps you could drop me off in town before you go to the shelter, and pick me up afterwards?" Jill asked.

Jack felt ashamed of himself again. It was boring for Jill to watch Jack ride horses all day. Of course she wanted a change of scenery!

"I'd be happy to."

All this being nice to everyone was cutting into his riding time: he would finish late tomorrow.

*

As Jack was driving Jill into town the next day on the way to the shelter to watch Robert, she said, "It's not going to work between us, is it, Jack?"

The question caught him off guard. "We live in different worlds now, Jill. You have your job in England, and I have my horse business out here."

"That's not exactly an obstacle to our being together."

"Granted. But we aren't the same people we were seventeen years ago." She couldn't argue with that!

"A lot of the way I am now is a direct result of what happened then, Jack. I was really hoping we could start all over again."

It was now clear to Jack that he had never been in love with her. He hadn't left Jill in the lurch because 'having a baby wasn't in the plan' or that he wasn't 'ready to get married yet.' He simply didn't want to marry *her*.

Nevertheless, he'd tenaciously held onto her image all these years as the only woman he knew who understood and was able to cope with his disease. While that might facilitate a relationship, it certainly wasn't the only criterion for a successful one.

And now, with her hating the Catholic Church which he had recently re-entered, what hope was there for them as a couple?

"We can talk about this tonight, Jill. But the short answer is, we're not compatible and I think deep down you know that."

Jill's eyes were filling up. Luckily Jack reached a convenient drop-off spot before the waterworks really kicked in.

"I'll pick you up back here in just over half an hour. O.K.?"

Jill nodded miserably and exited the vehicle.

He'd just dodged a bullet. She wouldn't dare cry with Robert in the car on his return.

At 11:30 precisely he showed up outside the dog shelter and parked near the entrance. It was another mild day, with a light breeze. He lowered the windows and waited for Robert to come out.

Barely two minutes later the youngster held the front door of the shelter open, and Jack could see a respectful Beckett sitting just inside the building until Robert gave him permission to walk out behind him.

That kid knew dogs! The similarities between dog training and horse training struck Jack again. Maybe he and Robert could discuss it sometime? It would bring their two animal interests together, and they could share useful information. This might be a way to begin that evangelization Father Michael wanted him to carry out.

Beckett and Robert walked past the Range Rover, and Jack waved at them.

"Hi! I want you to see how much better Beckett is on the leash than the first time you saw him."

Jack gave him the thumbs up. Watching them progress up the road, he had to acknowledge the huge improvement in the way the black dog kept pace with his handler. Instead of wandering all over the place and pulling, he padded softly along in rhythm with him.

Robert halted and asked the dog to carry out some commands. Beckett obeyed immediately. He lay down and rolled over, then got up again into the sitting position, and offered first his left then his right paw to Robert, who rewarded him for each action with a treat.

Jack was impressed.

The shelter was on a fairly quiet street, with few passers-by. In general Beckett didn't seem interested in the humans walking past, but suddenly raised his head as three people approached Robert.

Jack immediately recognized them as the bullies from that day outside Starbucks.

He groaned as they stopped in front of Robert and said something. For sure they were taunting him again. It was classic mob mentality: they had the advantage of numbers against the kid and Jack put his hand on the door handle, ready to jump out and intervene.

One of the boys pushed Robert's shoulder and Jack opened the door. But as he walked towards the group, he saw a change in Beckett.

The normally mild-mannered dog barred his teeth at the bully shoving his new buddy. The guy flinched then recovered. "Oh, your cute puppy is going to defend you, is he? We'll see about that! C'mon guys!"

But Robert said, "You *dare* touch my dog!" and Beckett snarled at the would-be attackers.

Jack halted. That dog had a fierce set of grinders that even he would have been afraid to mess with! He liked Robert's swift defense of the animal: the kid had developed a backbone.

His use of the term 'my dog' had not escaped Jack, either.

"Whoa, good doggie!" the bully cried. "I was only joking! Wasn't I, guys?" Retreating, he looked over his shoulder but his two friends had fled and he followed suit.

Beckett was back to his calm self and Robert knelt to hug him. "You *star* dog! Thank you! Thank you!"

Jack quietly came alongside.

The kid looked up at Jack: "I've *got* to adopt this dog!"

Your parents are going to kill me!

Chapter Nine: Church and a Fight

Preoccupied with this near-disaster, Jack almost forgot to pick Jill up on the way back to the farm. He shuddered to think of the scene she'd have made had he not remembered!

She was no longer crying, for which Jack was grateful, but neither did she go out of her way to talk to him. Instead she asked Robert questions about his morning.

Probably intended to hurt his feelings, her behavior actually made it easier for him to say to the two of them, "I'll have to ride for longer this afternoon, I'm afraid."

Jill shrugged her shoulders.

Robert said, "No problem, Mr. Jack."

"*Thank* you, Robert."

*

With the kid there, lunches for the next few days were at least civil, but dinners were torture. He was glad to seek the refuge of the cabin afterwards, with Katie instead of Jill for company.

He appreciated Robert's upbeat attitude and hard work all the more for their contrast with his ex-girlfriend's sulkiness. Once Jill was gone, he must get together with the kid and discuss dogs, horses and life.

Jill's icy demeanor continued through to Sunday, the day of her departure. Jack didn't enjoy having a moody person around and their parting would not be sorrowful.

Finally, Sunday morning arrived and Jack went to 8 a.m. Mass, leaving Jill at the farm house.

This was to be his first solo appearance in church. He no longer needed the support of his Mexican house keeper and her son and was glad to be alone.

There was a lot to chat to God about, and it was easier to do it in church without people around whom he knew.

He arrived early and slipped into a pew on the left side of the aisle, towards the front. Kneeling down he remembered that evening in England at the other Our Lady of Sorrows Church, at the vigil for his mother the day before her funeral.

He and his father had arrived first, with Jack feeling awkward and out of place.

Now he had a sense of belonging and someone to talk to about everything.

He had returned to his loving Father, Who embraces His children with all their faults and foibles. Jack was discovering that Catholicism goes well beyond rules and regulations and appearing to limit personal freedom.

Even the secular world acknowledges – in its saner moments – that freedom doesn't come free. Jack had learned that running from God is an exercise in futility and only obeying God's commandments brings true freedom.

Today evil was again flourishing: God was being ignored, set aside and ridiculed. Violence was on the rise and human life had become a commodity for others to use at will or extinguish altogether. Jack shuddered at the thought of how he had joined that culture when he told Jill to abort their baby.

Eliminating God was proving disastrous for the world. This 'enlightened' generation had learned nothing from the past, with many people considering the Bible to be pure fiction.

How could they believe that, when its veracity had been proven over and over again, often by those who sought to debunk it? It saddened Jack.

Yet, despite these considerations, he still harbored reservations about Catholicism. He wanted to embrace the Faith fully, but would be lying if he said he was completely on board with all aspects.

The ever-cheerful pastor had actually expressed relief that his new convert wasn't pretending to leap wholeheartedly into the religion, and had told Jack he'd be very suspicious had he done so.

Kneeling in the pew, Jack wished Jill would return to the faith of their childhood, too.

She was leaving this evening after a trip that had not been the reconciliation they'd hoped for.

And Jack's discoveries about his son were a mixed blessing, for in his darker moments he felt God was both rewarding and punishing him in equal measure.

Rewarding him for coming back to the Faith by letting him know that his son *didn't* die a brutal death under the abortionist's knife: punishing him for his selfish behavior towards the mother and child.

Ever since Jill revealed that their son had been adopted and she didn't know where he was or whether he was still alive, he'd been bottling up his emotions.

If he thought about it too long, he risked believing that God was not loving after all.

He risked believing that his return to the Faith had gained him nothing, that he hadn't really been forgiven and this whole religion thing was a sham. He needed to talk to Father Michael about this as soon as possible!

He immersed himself in the Mass and offered his Communion for Jill and their son.

After the service he was glad to see Father outside the church greeting his parishioners. He was popular, so the line was long. But Jack was in no hurry to get back to an irate Jill and patiently waited for his turn to shake the pastor's hand.

"Hello, Jack! Good to see you again! How are things?"

Not one for small talk, Jack got straight to the point. "Father, you know I mentioned having topics to discuss with you?"

"I've been looking forward to sparring with you on things Catholic."

"When would you have time?"

"Sounds serious, Jack. Normally I'd have you call the parish office and make an appointment, but I suspect it can't wait that long?"

Jack's eyes were unflinching. "No."

"I see. Tomorrow is my day off. Shall I come over to your place?"

"How about a healthy lunch – say at 12:30?"

"Done!" Father Michael shook Jack's hand firmly. He gave it a small squeeze and laid his other hand over it. "Courage, my friend."

Jack had the strong sensation of having just encountered Christ. What was the Church's Latin phrase to describe her priests? *In persona Christi* – that was it! "In the person of Christ."

Yes! That's exactly what he'd just experienced and hopefully its power would sustain him until the clergyman's visit tomorrow.

On Jack's return from church he and Jill ate a late breakfast alone. Felicia had left food in the fridge for them the evening before which the pair consumed in silence.

Jack's announcement "I've got to help Brad with the chores before we head out to Dulles," was welcomed by Jill. They needed a break from each other: the hour and a half trip to the airport was going to be bad enough.

And it was. Jill gave Jack the silent treatment all the way there and he gave her a perfunctory hug at the airport which she didn't return.

As the physical burden of her presence lifted, the emotional burden of guilt took its place. He was responsible for her leaving the Catholic Church and had rejected her a second time.

He looked forward to Father's company tomorrow and the return of his life to some sort of normalcy.

The Bluetooth lit up on his dashboard and his cell phone rang. He was thrilled to hear the voice on the other end.

"Hi, is that Mr. Jack?"

"Hey, is that you, Joe?"

"Sure is! How're you doing, sir?"

"All the better for hearing from you," he answered truthfully. "What's up?"

"Mom's been bugging me about coming to see you. She wants to meet and thank the man who turned her son's life around. You know what women are like."

Jack smiled at this 'guy talk' from the sixteen-year-old.

Son, I want to see you just as much as you want to see me. You don't have to hide behind your mother.

But he played along. "Sounds like we'd better let her come over, then." He paused. "You planning to come, too?" he teased.

"Of *course*! I can't let Mom make that trip alone!"

"How soon can you get here?"

When the conversation was over, Jack was in the best mood he'd been in for a long time.

Chapter Ten: Father Michael

The morning after his episode outside the shelter, a wildly excited Robert reported for duty at the farm full of praise for Beckett's actions.

"When I adopt him – "

"Whoa there, young man! Your dad is allergic to dogs, remember?"

"I'll figure something out. Anyway, I'm going to change his name to Reflex, because his reflex was to protect me when those bullies tried it on again." He paused for a moment. "Only I think I'll shorten it to 'Flex. What do you think?"

"I think you need to think harder about this." Jack had seen this coming, but with Jill around had relegated it to the back of his mind.

He'd taken the kid out of earshot of his ex-girlfriend. "Robert, I do understand your wanting to adopt Beckett – er, 'Flex – but it'll need some real thinking through, son. Can you leave it with me over the weekend? As soon as Ms. Penny has gone, we'll put our heads together. O.K.?"

The teenager had agreed.

But Jack returned to the farm on Sunday night elated after his call from Joe and having not given Robert's problem any thought at all.

Until Monday morning came around and he saw the boy's mother driving up to the barn to drop her son off. He knew Robert's first words would concern the dog.

"Hi, Mr. Jack! When can we have that talk?"

Thinking fast, Jack recalled he was getting a visit at midday from the person who'd asked him to take Robert on. Maybe a solution would present itself over their meal...

"I do have an idea," he said, half-truthfully, "but I can't talk to you about it until after lunch."

But Robert normally ate with him. How was he going to arrange to be alone with Father Michael?

"By the way, Father Michael is coming for lunch with me today. He's going to talk about religious stuff which you may not want to listen to. How about eating with Frank and Luca? They also get more interesting food than me."

The kid was enthusiastic about the plan.

"Good! Then I'll chat with you this afternoon about my idea."

The morning went by as usual, with Robert getting the mounts ready for Jack, Luca and Frank, and switching horses for the next shift so he could hose the sweaty ridden animals down and return them to their stalls.

Jack's first horse was Rustica and she was coming along well. Her transitions were much smoother and by asking her to engage her hind end into his soft hands, the mare was moving straighter and her head had stopped wagging from side to side in trot.

She struck off on both canter leads without throwing her nose in the air and her downward transitions to trot were quiet and in a round frame.

As Jack had predicted, her tongue no longer hung out of her mouth. By not focusing on the problem Jack had succeeded in eliminating it.[3]

She had three good paces and if Mrs. Payne took proper care of her, Rustica would make a good all-round horse and not revert to her former ways. As always, it depended on what the owner did with Jack's training.

Noon arrived and Robert went with the two men for lunch in the house attached to the barn, where Luca lived with his mother. Jack smiled at the kid's eagerness to go with his riders, sensing Robert saw this as validation that he really belonged to the team.

At Jack's request, Felicia had left food for him to eat with the priest without being disturbed.

---

[3] This is based on my own experience with an ex-racehorse who'd hung her tongue out for eighteen years before I got her. She stopped after relaxing into her new job as an eventer, without any intervention from me.

He'd just finished washing his hands in the kitchen basin and was drying them on the kitchen towel – since Felicia wasn't there to stop him – when Father Michael's blue sedan pulled up to the front porch.

Jack rapidly pulled the Saran wrap off the food on the table and walked out to meet his guest. Katie got to him first, running out of the house and down the porch steps.

"Hi, there, girl! Good to see you again."

The dog's tail wagged furiously, getting caught in the folds of his black soutane and rubbing golden hairs over it.

"Greetings to you, too, Jack!"

"Hello, Father! I see the welcoming committee has done its job."

"Yes, she has!"

"There's nothing like a good dog, is there?"

Jack's turn of phrase confused Father Michael, who responded with, "Dogs *are* great company, especially for people who live alone." He clearly hoped that was an appropriate response.

"Absolutely! Come on in, Father, lunch is served."

Jack poured them a glass of iced water each and sat down opposite his guest. "Shall we say grace?"

After the prayer, Father picked up his fork to start eating and Jack launched into his idea for Robert.

"Father, I appreciate your coming over on your day off. It's very good of you. And I do have some pressing spiritual issues to discuss.

"But before I start on those, I want to put a proposition to you – a practical one, not a spiritual one."

"I'm intrigued, Jack, do go on."

"You know how you asked me to take Robert on at the farm to help with his self-confidence?"

"Yes, and he seems to be doing very well. His mother called to say that after only two weeks he's already a stronger person."

"He's a valuable helper around the horses, and I'm glad to have him here. However, his real interest is not with equines, but canines. He'd much rather be working with dogs than here with me.

"I don't know if his mother told you, but Robert's also volunteering at the animal shelter in town, a couple of mornings a week. He's a genius with dogs."

"That must be improving his self-image, too."

"Yes, it is. But – as often happens when people work at shelters – he's found a dog he wants to adopt."

"That's marvelous!"

"Yes and no. His dad is allergic to dog hair, so he can't have one at home."

"Oh, dear, that *is* a shame."

"Yes, it is. But one particular animal actually saved him from the bullies who've been getting at him. I know, because I was there." Jack looked intently at the priest. "You can understand how an event like that would cement the bond between boy and dog, can't you?"

"Yes, I can."

"So I thought maybe you could help?"

"Me? How?" The clergyman stopped eating: Jack had his full attention.

"As you just said, a dog is a wonderful companion for people who live alone. So what do you say to adopting the dog for Robert?"

Father Michael blinked hard, several times.

Slyly, Jack continued. "Since you want Robert evangelized, what better way to do it than by adopting the dog on his behalf? It would encourage him to come and see you for spiritual direction."

The priest took a deliberately slow drink of water. "Jack, on the face of it that's a wonderful idea. But I simply don't have room for a dog. I live in a very small apartment, with no yard to speak of. I also have no idea how to look after one. The animal would be miserable with me."

Jack was disappointed. He'd really hoped the priest would appreciate the beauty of this plan. "Robert will be very upset, Father. I don't how to break it to him that he can't adopt the dog."

"You haven't told him you were going to ask me, have you?"

"No, I wasn't going to say anything just in case your answer was no."

The two of them ate in silence, and Jack could see his visitor thinking hard.

Halfway through his roast pork, Father said, "How about this for a plan?"

"I'm all ears."

"What would you say to my adopting the dog but having it live here with you?"

It was Jack's turn to blink. "How would *that* work?"

"I'll pay the adoption fee and for the dog's food. You have room for another dog, and Robert can see him every day when he comes to the farm."

"That is possible – in *theory*. But only until Robert goes back to school, which is in a few weeks. What then?"

"Hmmm... Would you let Robert come and visit the dog on the weekends or in the evenings?"

Jack felt he was being taken advantage of and said as much to the priest, who replied, "Why don't we go ahead with the adoption, and I'll find a parish family to take him once school begins?

"That way, Robert will have his dog before it gets adopted by someone else, and he'll be able to spend all day with it while he's working for you. What do you say?"

Jack thought about this idea. "If I agree to this , Father, you have to *promise* me you'll find someone else to keep the dog after school starts."

"You have my word, Jack, even if he has to sleep in cramped quarters with me until I sort out a new home for him."

"O.K. we'll tell Robert the good news after lunch. But now I want to discuss another issue."

He explained about having phoned Jill, per his penance, and how she'd told him 'there's a lot more to it.' How their time together this past week had only highlighted their differences and she'd left in bitterness.

"She abandoned the faith because of what I did, Father, and laughs at it – and at me for returning to it. I'm dealing with a mixture of extreme guilt and anger."

"I see, Jack. Anything else?"

"She did finally tell me that she'd never had the abortion."

"That's wonderful!"

"Yes, Father, but she put our son up for adoption."

The pastor nodded. "That must be hard for you."

"Very. It happened in England and was a closed adoption, so Jill has no idea who the parents are, or even whether our son is still alive, or where he would be if he is."

The priest sat back and folded his hands on his black garbed lap. "She gave you a good deal to think about, didn't she?"

"You can say that again! It's as if God has rewarded me for coming back to Him by letting me know I'm not responsible for my son's abortion. Yet He's also punishing me because I abandoned Jill and told her to terminate the pregnancy."

"Why do you think that?"

Isn't it obvious? "Because He won't let me know where my son is or if he's even still alive. And He's making me feel responsible for Jill leaving the Church."

"You're placing an unfair burden on God, Jack."

"What do you mean?"

"You're attributing to God thoughts and actions that aren't His, and placing responsibility for events on the wrong person."

"*Excuse* me?"

The priest continued calmly: "Remember telling me how frustrated you get with owners who cause their horses' problems then expect you to fix them?"

Jack nodded slowly.

"And how you get annoyed because the owners blame the animals for the negative results of their actions and don't take responsibility as they should?"

Jack had a good idea where the clergyman was going with this. "You're saying that God gave us free will, and we shouldn't blame God when we use it to create bad situations in our lives?"

"Bravo! That's *exactly* what I'm saying." He quickly raised his hands in a conciliatory gesture. "But you didn't ask me here to tell you it's your fault things aren't going well, so let's dwell on the positive. Your son *didn't* die, despite your intentions. In His infinite mercy, God intervened and changed Jill's mind about the abortion.

"And how did you discover all this? By coming back to your faith – again, through the mercy of God.

"As for Jill's reaction to Catholicism and your return to the faith: don't let it bother you. She has her own journey to make and God will help her along it. But it *was* important for you to spend time together, otherwise you'd have continued wondering whether things might have worked between you."

Jack nodded thoughtfully.

"Now you can be certain that the relationship would never have survived had you married. Your son is happier being adopted and raised in a loving home than with a mother and father who don't get on and would have fought all the time – probably ending up getting divorced."

Jack stared at his hands, trying to take in this new point of view.

Father Michael smiled. "I always say it's better not to get married at all than to try and get unmarried. Let Jill's decision to keep her baby be enough for you and don't beat yourself up over her leaving the church."

He wasn't quite finished. "And don't blame God for the way the adoption worked out. Thank Him instead for making sure your wishes didn't prevail. God bailed you out, Jack, He's not 'making you pay.' What you can usefully do is pray for Jill and for your son."

Jack appreciated the truth of the priest's words. He *had* been blaming God for the outcomes in his life, just like the horse owners he so scorned. Father Michael's analogy explained events in way to which he could relate, and Jack felt more at peace with the situation.

What an astute man he had for a pastor!

"Thank you, Father. Now, about this dog…"

Chapter Eleven: A New Home for 'Flex

That discussion with Father Michael had lifted a huge burden off Jack – at least regarding Jill.

It was great not to have someone watch him ride during the day, making him aware of his failings as a host, and he relished the freedom of his house in the evening.

Robert was overjoyed that Father Michael was willing to adopt 'Flex and that the dog would stay at Jack's farm.

"Mr. Jack," he said on their ride back from the shelter that Tuesday morning, "'Flex can't wait to come back with us tomorrow! You should have seen him wagging his tail when I told him!"

"You did remember to tell the shelter staff, too – not just the dog, right?"

Robert grimaced. "Of course, I did! They'll have the paperwork ready for Father Michael to sign tomorrow morning."

That night, after saying his prayers, Jack thought of the black dog with the white tipped tail reacting positively to the news of his impending release from the shelter.

Katie's life was going to change, too. How would she cope with a new dog around? She'd been by herself for so many years! Would she understand if he explained their plans to her, as 'Flex allegedly had?

He doubted it, but it was worth a shot.

The Golden Retriever lay next to him on the bed and he stroked her silky head. Her hair was still growing back after being shaved off a few weeks ago while Joe was here, so her head and tail were the only areas with the original soft feel to them.

"Katie, you're going to have a male canine companion as of tomorrow. He's a great dog, and he isn't mine – so don't get upset. He'll belong to Robert, via Father Michael, and with luck won't be here beyond the beginning of the school year.

"It's a temporary deal, O.K.?"

The dog's sleepy eyes barely cracked open to receive this information. Hoping she'd be as laid back when 'Flex arrived, Jack switched off the bedside table light.

Tomorrow would worry about itself, as the Bible says.

*

The next morning at 9 a.m. Father arrived promptly at Jack's farm, having said the 8 a.m. Mass.

Robert was hard at work, grooming as many horses as he could for Luca and Frank to exercise while Jack was with him at the shelter.

The horse trainer's morning absence would make his day longer than usual. But Robert had promised to stay until all the horses were ridden and washed down, all the feeds distributed and every animal turned out for the night. That was his end of the bargain, and Jack was confident the lad would stick to it.

Father Michael climbed into the front passenger seat of Jack's pick-up and Robert sat in the back with a blanket he'd brought from home.

"This is 'Flex's," he announced. "I'll get him some more stuff this weekend. But he can sleep on this to start."

His eyes were bright with excitement and he thanked the priest profusely for adopting the dog on his behalf. Father Michael pumped him with questions about his new canine, and Robert happily supplied the answers.

The lady at the front desk of the dog shelter was surprised to see a man in a black soutane and white dog collar enter the building.

Robert explained, "This is Father Michael, who is going to adopt 'Flex – I mean, Beckett – for me."

The pastor shook the lady's hand. "Don't worry, I haven't come to administer the Last Rites to any of your canine residents."

Jack and Robert laughed, but confusion covered the lady's face again.

Jack enlightened her. "That's the Catholic sacrament administered to the terminally ill, usually just before they die."

"Oh, I see." She still with no idea what they meant but *had* grasped the important fact that this strange man was here to adopt a dog.

"So, you're interested in Beckett? Did I understand that correctly?" Her eyes were filled with optimism. "He's a great dog and Robert has done wonders with him."

The priest put her mind at rest. "I don't need persuading, Ms. ? – "

"Oh, I'm Mrs. Thurston. And you are - ?"

"Father Michael. Now what do I need to do to adopt Beckett?"

"Don't you want to see the dog first?"

Robert chimed in. "Let me show him to you, Father."

Jack smiled: it reminded him of every time he bought a new horse and couldn't wait to see the animal.

The priest obliged. "Absolutely! I'd love to see my new dog."

"Would you come with me, Robert, and we'll bring him out?" Mrs. Thurston asked.

Five minutes later Robert appeared with the black animal on a leash. He asked the dog to sit next to him, and Beckett instantly complied. "Say 'hello' to Father Michael, your new owner!"

The priest knelt down in front of the dog, and Robert said, "Paw!"

A white-tipped paw lifted off the ground and the clergyman took it gently in his hand. "Hello, there! Are you ready to come home with us?"

Beckett put his head to one side as if trying to comprehend as this new human stroked his head and stood up. Robert told the dog to lie down.

Again, the response was immediate.

Father Michael turned to Mrs. Thurston, who had taken her position behind the desk again. With a big grin he said, "I'll take him!"

As if there'd been any doubt! Jack thought.

Robert made a whooping sound. "You won't regret this, I promise you!"

Fifteen minutes later the paperwork was complete, and a proud Robert led the priest's new dog out of the shelter.

The youngster sat next to Beckett on the back seat of the pickup with his left arm around the dog and a big smile on his face. "Mr. Jack, thank you so much! This is great! I have my own – er – Father Michael's dog to train! I'll be over every single day to take care of him!"

"You're welcome, Robert, and I don't doubt that you *will* be over every single day."

When the truck pulled up at the farm house Katie came bounding over.

"Robert, how about if I get out first with Father? We'll make a fuss of her before you introduce 'Flex."

Two minutes later Robert got out and greeted Katie, leaving Beckett in the vehicle. "I've got someone who wants to meet you."

To Jack and the priest he said, "We have to let them sniff each other without holding onto them. If we keep 'Flex on a tight leash he'll feel anxious and get aggressive. So we have to stay very calm and give them plenty of room to get used to each other. I can grab 'Flex if anything goes wrong."

Jack was impressed with the kid for taking control. "It's your call, Robert. You're the dog person."

"O.K.! C'mon, 'Flex," Robert's voice was low and neutral.

The black dog jumped down from the truck and Katie padded over to him. Both canines' tails were wagging as they sniffed each other's rear ends. Soon Katie was adopting the front paws down, butt in the air pose that indicates a desire to play. Her tail continued to wag furiously.

'Flex looked back at Robert as if asking permission to have fun. "Sure, boy!"

The black animal mimicked Katie's posture and they danced around each other for a while before 'Flex ran off with Katie giving chase.

The two dogs raced in large circles around the three men. The Retriever wasn't fast enough to catch up with the mixed breed and eventually 'Flex stood still to let her catch up with him. They flopped down in the driveway next to each other.

Father Michael laughed. "I think those two will get along just fine."

Jack privately agreed, but said quietly, "Yes, for the short period 'Flex will be here." He didn't want the priest forgetting to find his dog a new location come the fall semester.

It was said out of earshot of Robert as the two adults hadn't yet explained that this farm arrangement wasn't for the long term. They would tell him only when the next home had been found for the dog.

"By the way, Robert, why do you call him 'Flex?" the pastor asked. "I thought his name was Beckett?"

"His reflex was to protect me when the bullies went after me again. So 'Flex is short for reflex – it's easier to say than 'Reflex.'"

The priest nodded. "That's a good reason and a good name for your canine defender."

"Well, *your* defender, Father."

"Robert, we all know whose dog this really is."

"Does that mean I can tell people that he's my dog?"

"Certainly does, son."

The kid grinned.

Given the later ending to their work day as a result of picking up the dog, Robert was going to eat dinner with Jack.

Father said, "If you like, I can come back later and pick Robert up to take him home. It'll give me a chance to see how Robert's new dog is settling in."

"Only if you join us for dinner at around 7:30, Father."

"O.K. Jack, you've twisted my arm."

The horse trainer stood with the priest and Robert for a few minutes, watching 'Flex take off again, unable to believe his luck at coming to such a beautiful new home with so much room to run around in.

"Perhaps the dog will evangelize Robert," Jack said, walking the clergyman back to his car.

Father Michael raised a sardonic eyebrow. "Just because 'dog' is 'God' spelled backwards doesn't mean this animal lets either you or me off the hook for reeling this boy into a relationship with the Lord."

Chapter Twelve: Joe's Return

That first night Jack knelt to pray with not one but two dogs lying next to him.

'Flex began by sleeping on his blanket on the bedroom floor. But Jack wasn't surprised when a black form jumped up next to Katie soon after he climbed into bed. He awoke the next morning wedged between the gold and ebony forms.

Yesterday evening, with Father Michael looking on, Robert had demonstrated how to feed the two dogs. He made each one sit and wait while he placed their bowls of chow at a short distance from them, with the water dish in the middle.

"It'll save them fighting over food," he said.

This morning Jack was pleased when Katie and 'Flex listened to his command to sit while he put their dishes on the floor. Then he waved his hand towards the food as permission for them to eat, and they rushed over with gusto.

He had brought 'Flex's blanket from the bedroom and placed it near Katie's bed in the kitchen. Once they'd finished eating and inspected the other's bowls in case something had been left in them, Jack motioned to them to lie down in their respective places.

Felicia's first comment on meeting 'Flex yesterday had been, "He big dog, Master Robert!" and she kept a wide berth.

"But he's a very *gentle* dog," he'd reassured her. "And very well trained."

"Mmmm!" had been her response.

But when she witnessed the two dogs sitting quietly, awaiting Jack's permission to eat their breakfast, she'd visibly relaxed around the canine newcomer.

"I think we've done a good thing in letting Robert have this dog," Jack said.

"No look to me like Master Robert have this dog," was her shrewd observation.

"Have you made up the beds for Master Joe and his mother yet?" Jack retorted. "Don't forget, they're arriving this afternoon."

Just then Robert's mother pulled up in the Camry and her son leapt out, calling to his dog.

Mrs. Riceman exited her vehicle and shook Jack's hand. "I can't thank you enough for letting Robert have this dog, Mr. Harper. He's so excited, and it's the next best thing to having one at home. I just wish his father were able to tolerate canine hair."

"I should have suggested Robert get a hairless dog!"

"Is there such a thing?"

"Yes, but I think they look rather odd. Robert would have been well and truly teased if he had one of those. And anyway, I doubt whether you'd find one in a shelter. As I understand, they're pretty rare."

"Well, since he has a normal haired dog I so appreciate your keeping him at your farm. We'll compensate you for it, of course."

"Don't worry. Father Michael is paying for his food and vets' bills, so I'm not out of pocket."

"He's being so kind!"

Jack nodded. "He's a very good man."

"Yes, he is. How did things go on 'Flex's first night?"

"The dogs had a grand time squashing me between them on the bed."

"Oh, I do apologize, Mr. Harper. That's terrible! Robert needs to train his dog to stay off the bed!"

"It's fine, Mrs. Riceman. I'll survive."

"No, I'll get Robert to make him sleep on the floor!"

"It's actually not fair to allow Katie to sleep with me while he can't. Leave it as it is, I really don't mind."

Whoa, Jack! In the old days you'd have insisted otherwise!

Robert was playing fetch with both dogs. He paused to wave goodbye to his mother as she got back into the Toyota, and told

'Flex, "C'mon, boy, let's get to work. I have some horses you need to meet!" And off he went, followed by both dogs.

Once her son was out of earshot, Mrs. Riceman leaned out of the car window. "Thank you for all you've done, Mr. Harper. My son is so self-assured and happy. Father Michael did tell me it would happen, but I was skeptical."

Jack smiled. That priest should have been a psychologist instead of a clergyman. "Robert is a valuable worker who also has a talent with dogs. He's found his niche, there, Mrs. Riceman."

She sighed. "I don't know if there's any money to be made in dog training, but I sure hope so."

"If I can make money in horse training, he can definitely earn a living with dogs. I wouldn't worry about it. I started out working on one horse, and look where it led me. Once he's trained 'Flex – and he's already been successful with Katie – he'll be looking for other dogs to help. It'll grow from here, like it did with me."

"Do you really think so?"

"Yes. Let him follow his passion and he'll never work a day in his life, as the saying goes. *And* he'll gain respect as he becomes an expert in his field."

"When you put it that way, I feel bad that we've never been able to have a dog at home."

"Well, 'Flex has a home here for now."

"That's very generous of you, Mr. Harper. We owe you a lot."

"Not at all, Mrs. Riceman. Have a great day, and I'll see you this afternoon."

Throughout the day Jack noticed Robert keeping the dog under his watchful eye. When he was handling the horses, he tied 'Flex in the barn with a bowl of water and a saddle blanket to lie on where the animal could watch and get used to horses walking back and forth without feeling he had to get up and defend himself from the huge animals and their big feet.

Katie lay next to him, helping the newbie stay calm. Soon he would also be off leash.

Joe and his mother were due around 4 p.m. that afternoon and Jack was determined to have all the horses exercised, fed and turned out before they arrived.

He'd originally wanted Robert gone by then – but why? Did he want Joe to himself? If so, how absurd! He was confident the two boys would get on, so why shouldn't they meet straight away?

As it turned out, the point became moot: Robert's mother called to apologize because she would be half an hour late picking up her son.

Jack didn't have time to shower after riding that afternoon, but cleaned himself up in the kitchen sink, so he could look out of the window for Joe's arrival. It would be good to see him again!

Had the kid bulked up at all in the few weeks since leaving the farm?

Jack wanted to hear how Duke was behaving and whether Joe had taken him to any competitions in that short time.

He was drying his face on the kitchen towel, hoping Felicia wouldn't notice, when he saw an unfamiliar black Expedition come up the drive with a Virginia license plate. They must be Joe and his mother.

With no time to check in the mirror, he drew his hands through his unruly blond hair and walked onto the porch.

But before he reached the steps, Joe had already leaped out of the SUV and was running over to greet him.

"Mr. Jack!" he yelled.

Jack put out his arms and the teenager gave him an enormous hug. He squeezed the kid tightly and over Joe's shoulder could see his mother smiling broadly as she exited her car.

He took a sharp breath. Something about her immediately attracted him – but he couldn't pinpoint what.

Her shoulder length black hair was held behind each ear with a clasp, but the natural curls resented being restrained. It was impossible not to compare this petite lady with the taller and stouter Jill.

She hesitated to introduce herself, not wanting to interfere in her son's reunion with the man who'd exerted such a strong and positive influence on him.

Jack considered waving to her to come over but decided against it. That was Joe's job.

"Mom! Come say 'hi'!"

Joe walked to the vehicle. "Come and meet the famous Mr. Jack Harper, Mom!" He grabbed her hand.

Jack was suddenly embarrassed. "Not *that* famous."

A warm smile brightened her face, highlighting her deep blue eyes and long black lashes. "I'm afraid I have to disagree, Mr. Harper. In our household at least, you are *enormously* famous. You're my son's hero."

Joe looked a little sheepish at this comment and Jack put his hand on the boy's shoulder. "I don't know about that, but we had a lot of fun together, didn't we, son?"

It suddenly occurred to him that his mother might find the term 'son' over familiar.

But Mrs. Ross said, "I can understand why Joe felt so relaxed here. He was obviously accepted as part of the family."

Robert exited the barn with the dogs and Joe cried, "There you are, Katie! C'm'ere, girl!" The dog rushed over to him.

"Thank you for keeping the dogs out of the way." Jack turned to Joe and his mother. "Robert is helping me with the horses. This is Mrs. Ross and her son, Joe, who brought his horse, Duke to me a few weeks ago."

Robert shook Mrs. Ross's hand.

"Nice to meet you," she said as Joe stood up from petting the Golden Retriever.

The teenagers eyed each other, reminding Jack of the two dogs' first meeting. But unlike with the canines, he had less confidence in his assumption that the boys would instantly hit it off.

Katie looked up at Joe with adoring eyes and an alert 'Flex sat next to Robert.

Then both canines suddenly began wagging their tails: the barn cat had appeared from under the porch. On catching sight of the dogs, he bounded towards the barn and they set off after him.

Joe cried, "Hey, Katie, come back!"

"'Flex! You bad dog, git back here!" Robert yelled, as both boys took off after their animals.

Jack laughed. "Well, I guess they'll be gone for a while. Would you like to come in for some iced water or tea? Or we could sit on the porch and keep an eye out for the boys. Or would you prefer me to bring in your luggage and show you to your room, first?" He reddened. Where was this barrage of nervous questions coming from?

Laughter lines appeared under Mrs. Ross's deep blue eyes and her smile was gentle. "I'd love some iced tea, please. And sitting out here sounds perfect. You have such a lovely place!"

"Thank you. And please, take a seat," Jack pointed to the wicker chairs around the table on the porch, with their blue and white striped cushions. "I'll be right out."

As he rummaged in the kitchen for two tall glasses and poured out iced tea for Mrs. Ross and iced water for himself, Jack continued to puzzle over his weird behavior.

He placed a glass in front of his guest.

"Would you like something to eat?" he inquired.

"Only if you're able to share it with me. I'm really not that hungry, but I expect you are."

It took him a split second to understand. Then – of course! Her son had ulcerative colitis, too, so she fully grasped the ramifications of the disease.

How refreshing not to have to pretend in front of her. "Actually, yes, I am hungry. It's been a long afternoon. I'll fetch something we can both eat."

"Not your chocolate chip bread, by any chance?"

How did she know about that? *Because, you dummy, Joe loved eating it and took the recipe home!*

"Have you made it?" he asked.

"I know that recipe off by heart!"

Jack shook his head. "Sorry about that."

"Don't be. And if you *were* planning to eat some, I'll gladly join you."

"You're on!"

Two minutes later he reappeared with a loaf of the bread, a knife, two small plates and a couple of napkins.

"Voilà! Home from home."

"Let's see if it's as good as mine."

Jack cut her a slice and handed the plate to her. "That's a given."

She shook her head. "I doubt it."

The boys returned. Dragging themselves behind were the two dogs, panting furiously with their tongues hanging out.

"I'll get their water bowl," Robert said.

"K.," Joe said, eyeing the food. "Hey, is that what I think it is?"

"Yup!" Jack said. "Would you fetch a couple more plates from the kitchen, please? And get yourselves something to drink."

As Joe disappeared after Robert, Jack commented, "Looks like the two of them are getting along well."

"This farm seems to have that effect on people."

Unsure what she meant and painfully aware that it hadn't been the case with him and Jill, Jack settled for, "It would be great if that were true."

Soon Joe and Robert were sitting next to each other on the porch swing, sipping iced water and snacking on chocolate chip bread. Katie and 'Flex were sprawled out on the white floor boards, next to the water bowl which Robert had already refilled once.

The teens were telling Jack and Mrs. Ross about their cat chase when Mrs. Riceman's Toyota came into view.

"Robert, your mother's here," Jack said.

'Flex's new owner gave a big sigh and Jack understood. The last half hour had been fun and it was hard for the kid to leave their little group.

He rose and walked down the porch steps to meet the vehicle ahead of Robert.

"At the risk of kidnapping your son, Mrs. Riceman," he said through the driver's window, "would you mind if Robert brought his overnight things with him tomorrow? A former client and his mother are visiting, and it might be fun for your son to stay after work and hang out with him. They're the same age, and seem to get on well."

Mrs. Riceman peered through the windshield at her son sitting with Joe and the dogs on the porch.

"It's good for Robert to socialize with kids his age. And to be honest, it would mean his dad and I could go out to dinner. We haven't been out on our own for a long time."

"Can I take that as a yes?"

"If you're happy spending even more time with him, then I'm happy for him to stay over tomorrow night. I'll see that he brings his things."

Jack nodded and waved to Robert, who was dragging his feet down the steps with 'Flex. "Hey, your mum's waiting, young man!"

The boy hurried.

"We'll see you tomorrow, Robert. Your mother will fill you in on the details."

"What details?"

"Hop in and I'll tell you on the way home," said his mother. "Good bye, Mr. Harper!"

"Bye 'Flex!" Robert called.

Mrs. Riceman growled, "How about saying 'bye' to Mr. Harper?"

"Thank you, Mr. Jack! Good bye!"

Dinner that evening was a relaxed affair, as Jack had no need to make apologies for the food to Mrs. Ross. Since Joe's conversion to the protocol for ulcerative colitis sufferers, this was the same fare she ate when visiting her son at her brother's farm, where he was currently living.

Joe had moved there after his father died and the ulcerative colitis kicked in. His mother felt he would do better in the country with plenty of outdoor pursuits, rather than cooped up in their Richmond apartment.

Felicia was overjoyed to see Joe again. "You no skinny boy no more!"

"Nope, Ms. Felicia. Thanks to your cooking and my keeping to the diet, I've put on about five pounds. And every week I put on more!"

Joe's tact in giving credit to Felicia's cooking brought home the fact that Jack himself never did so.

"You're a genius at making a restricted diet taste great," Mrs. Ross added. "I need to take notes."

Over the meal Jack enjoyed listening to Joe's stories about Duke and the three of them ended the evening back out on the porch.

Joe sat in the swing chair with Katie and 'Flex by his feet. Jack noticed the black dog's front right paw touching his Golden Retriever's left paw, and neither cared. It boded well for the future.

It was half past eight and the sun was setting behind the house, throwing an eerie glow across the sky. Nobody wanted to get up, so they chatted about this and that until it got dark and the midges came out.

When a mosquito landed in his iced water, Jack said, "Time for me to turn in. I have to get up early to bring the horses in." He winked at Joe. "Are you going to help me with them or lie idly in bed tomorrow morning?"

He looked at the youngster, who was turning seventeen in December. He had indeed filled out since they last saw each other and developed more muscle. It was great that he was staying in remission. And his skin was normal, too. All good signs.

Mrs. Ross looked at her son, and there was such love in her eyes!

Mum must have looked at me like that, but I never paid attention.

Joe grinned at Jack. "Depends on how I feel and when I wake up!"

"I'll take that as a 'yes, you can't wait to help me' then."

Joe laughed. "Yessir!"

Mrs. Ross made a move to get up but Jack said, "Don't come in on my account."

"I'm tired, too," she said. "It's been a long week at work and this country air is making me sleepy."

"Me too, Mom. C'mon Katie, c'mon 'Flex."

Jack bade both his guests goodnight and watched Katie follow Joe to his room. He smiled: it was just like old times.

Mrs. Ross exchanged a glance with him that said, *Joe and that dog..!* before she, too, walked down the hallway to her room.

'Flex was sitting next to Jack with a confused expression. Jack pointed at Joe's disappearing back. "Go on, I shan't be upset with you!" but the black animal stayed by his side. "O.K. Looks like I've swapped a golden dog for a dark one. Come on, then."

'Flex padded behind him into the master bedroom.

Chapter Thirteen: Mrs. Ross

Jack rose early the next morning to begin his chores at 6 a.m., and pulled a quick snack from the fridge.

Felicia would serve breakfast to his visitors later and he might pop back in for more food. Ulcerative colitis sufferers are always ravenous!

It took just over an hour for him and his two men to distribute feed and hay, bring in the horses and fill their water buckets. At 7:30 Robert would arrive and help prepare the few horses on today's roster.

He looked at his watch: there was luckily time for another bite before the kid's arrival.

Joe and his mother were sitting around the kitchen table when he entered. Felicia was serving gluten-free pasta lightly grilled in olive oil with fried zucchini, green peppers and bacon.

She had also made coconut flour pancakes. On the table were maple syrup and blueberry flavored and strawberry flavored coconut yogurts. Joe had developed a passion for them during his time on the farm earlier that summer and was presently tucking into one.

"Good morning!" Jack said.

Joe waved at him. "Hi, Mr. Jack!"

Mrs. Ross smiled, revealing a slightly uneven upper tooth. "Good morning, Mr. Harper. This is a great breakfast spread!"

I wonder whether I can tell her to call me 'Jack'? Is that being too forward?

"I told you Ms. Felicia is a genius with my – er, our – food, Mom!"

The glowing house keeper spooned more of the pasta onto the teenager's plate, amusing her employer. She was so easy to soft-soap.

"Thanks!"

Jack took a dish out of the cupboard and stood next to her. "Please, ma'am, may I have some, too?"

The Mexican shook her head. "Good ting I make so much food today!"

"Yup!" He grinned exaggeratedly as she piled his plate high with the fried mixture.

He sat with Joe and Mrs. Ross and talked about his plans for the day. "I do have to work with some horses till noon. But then I thought we could take lunch down to the cabin. What do you think?"

"Will Robert be here?" asked Joe.

"Sure. He wants to spend as much time as possible with 'Flex. We'll take both dogs with us."

While they were chatting, Robert showed up before his scheduled time. It must have been hard for him knowing Joe was at the house overnight with Katie while he had to go home without his new dog.

The kid stood on the porch by the front door. "Knock, knock!" he said loudly. Two weeks ago, he'd not have had the confidence to do that.

"Come in!" Joe shouted, rising from the table as Katie and 'Flex leapt up from the cool floor tiles.

His mother admonished him. "Joe! This is not your house! It's not up to you to invite Mr. Harper's visitors in! And what do you say when you want to leave the table?"

When can I tell her not to call me Mr. Harper?

The kid turned around and apologized.

"It's O.K., son. Tell him to come in and join us."

The two adults heard Joe welcome Robert, who greeted both dogs.

"We're going to have lunch at the cabin today," Joe said.

"What cabin?"

"You haven't seen the cabin yet? It's real cool - and you can fish in the lake. We're taking the dogs, too."

Jack smiled to himself. He'd taken Joe down to the cabin after the kid's mishap with his horse during training. Stress had brought on another ulcerative colitis flare and Jack was desperate to get Joe's mind off the accident. The lake was at the back of his property, and they'd fished for several hours without catching anything, yet Joe clearly recalled that afternoon with fondness.

Robert said, "Good morning, Mrs. Ross."

"Good morning, Robert. Are you helping Mr. Harper with the horses this morning?"

I do wish she'd stop calling me that!

"Yes," the boy said proudly. "I groom them and tack them up and take care of them when he's finished riding."

"I really couldn't do without you now," Jack said.

The kid reddened slightly but looked pleased.

Joe said stoutly, "I'm coming to help, too."

"That *was* the deal." Jack looked over at Mrs. Ross. "But only if your mum doesn't mind. What's she going to do while you're with me?"

Her response was quick. "I'll sit in the bleachers and watch you ride."

"Are you sure you won't be bored?" he said.

"I doubt that very much." Those eyes were smiling at him again.

"O.K. Then we'll be off to the barn."

Jack left with the two boys and the two dogs.

Luca and Frank gave the thumbs up when they saw two helpers instead of one.

"Alright!" Luca said. "We'll get through our morning in double quick time with you two on board!" He pointed at Robert, "Could you get Goliath ready? Joe, can you remember where everything is?"

"'Course, Mr. Luca!"

"Great, then could you tack up Rolando?"

While Joe and Robert groomed their two horses, Jack brushed Rustica. He believed that consistent handling from one person would increase the mare's trust and calm her. Before she went home, Luca and Frank would ride her to make sure she really had settled down.

While he and the boys were at work in the barn, Luca and Frank set up some gymnastic jumps in the outdoor arena. The three horses were going to be schooled through low jump grids.

At least that'll give Mrs. Ross something interesting to watch, Jack thought.

He led Rustica out, followed by Joe and Robert with Rolando and Goliath.

The boys handed their charges to Luca and Frank. Jack told them, "Go keep your mum company, Joe. Robert, I'll need your help in the ring shortly. And keep the dogs under control, O.K.?"

They walked their canines up the bleacher steps and sat next to Mrs. Ross while the three trainers mounted up and rode into the large sand arena.

Jack had never been concerned about what people thought of his riding, but suddenly became self-conscious.

The final jump grid would consist of a trot pole in front of a cross pole, one canter stride to an upright and another single canter stride to a small oxer.

At present only the trot pole and cross pole were ready. The stands for the vertical and oxer were in place, waiting for the poles lying on either side to be laid in the cups.

For the first ten minutes, the three men warmed up their horses in walk, trot and canter. Luca then took his horse over the cross pole, followed by Frank. Jack would go last on the more excitable Rustica.

Rolando and Goliath kept an even, active trot over the pole on the ground then onto the little fence, and continued in a controlled canter on a straight line after it.

Rustica, on the other hand, became hot as soon as she saw the poles. She tossed her head and tucked her nose into her chest, erratically flicking out her front hooves.

Jack had to turn her away several times and establish a regular trot tempo before attempting the tiny jump.

This wasn't the first horse he'd ridden that needed calming down before a jump. It wasn't a big deal and normally he wouldn't care.

Yet today it mattered very much to him that the mare trot quietly over that cross pole. And because it was important to him, he tensed up. The mare became more agitated and darted sideways.

He felt Luca and Frank looking on with puzzlement.

With some difficulty, Jack brought the chestnut to a halt, loosened the reins and gently scratched her withers. He shook his head and avoided the looks of his staff. "It's not you, girl, it's me," he muttered.

She calmed down and stretched out her nose with a long sigh.

Inhaling deeply, Jack cantered around the arena on a light contact. He transitioned into a rhythmic trot before lining her up again for the cross pole.

To Jack's immense relief the mare flowed smoothly over it.

He called up to Robert, who climbed down from the bleachers and placed the pole in the jump cups for the vertical fence.

This time all three horses jumped obediently over both obstacles.

Robert then built the oxer. Rolando was the first to go through the whole fence grid, and tried to duck out of the last fence. Luca clamped his legs on the gelding's side and the animal made an awkward leap over it.

Luca laughed and stroked the horse's neck. "Scaredy cat!"

Goliath popped over all three fences without a second glance. After the enormous heights he'd been forced to jump as a young horse, he found this work easy and fun. Jack smiled to see the horse's rehabilitation working so well.

It was now his turn to take the mare through the grid. She became a little hot again at the sight of the oxer at the far end of the grid, but Jack was able to guide her through with no problem. *Phew!*

He asked Robert to take the horse blanket draped over the arena fence and place it over the front pole of the oxer, to make it look different and keep everyone on their toes. The bright blue, red and yellow pattern did make the jump look spooky.

Rolando backed off as he approached the weird last fence, but – with strong encouragement from Frank – took off from a deep spot that just missed being a refusal.

His rider returned to the other two and rolled his eyes. *"That was close!"*

Goliath didn't bat an eyelid. This was pure recreation for him.

It was now Jack's turn. He cantered Rustica calmly around the arena, brought her back to trot and asked for active engagement.

As he turned towards the grid, his heart went into overdrive. *This is just a stupid, tiny grid, for Goodness' sake!*

Aware of all eyes on him, he sent up a quick prayer for help.

Rising into the two point position, he looked straight ahead and slowed down his breathing. They reached the trot pole on a good stride, and Rustica quietly popped over the cross pole into a balanced canter towards the upright.

But Jack felt her body tense underneath him when she spotted the blanket over the third jump. She prepared to stop at the second fence already.

He sat deep into the saddle and squeezed both legs on her sides.

Don't you dare let me down, girl!

Rustica made an awkward jump over the upright and almost halted in front of the blanket-covered oxer.

For her pains she received another strong press on her flanks and a loud clucking sound from Jack.

You are not weaseling out of this, horse!

She had indeed planned to scoot out to the left. But Jack made it impossible for her and she lunged at the oxer from a standstill.

The spread between the front and back poles was small, but the petite chestnut sailed over the oxer as though it were massive, clearing it by a full 24 inches in her determination not to touch the scary blanket.

She landed a long way off on the other side and Jack quickly righted himself in the saddle. It was his turn to join the others with a silly grin on his face, vaguely aware of clapping in the bleachers.

"That horse can jump, Jack!" Luca said.

"I wish I'd got that on my phone," Robert added.

Jack patted Rustica lightly on her neck. "It wasn't much of a test of her ability – but not a bad beginning, either," he admitted.

"Think maybe we should jump her a bit more?" Luca suggested.

Jack wasn't a fan of jumping horses too often. "As long as we keep it fun and not strenuous."

While the three men walked their horses off around the arena, he forced himself not to look up at his spectators. That would be uncool.

Only when Joe called out, "That was awesome!" did he have a legitimate reason to see how that little display had affected Mrs. Ross.

Chapter Fourteen: Down at the Cabin

The last horse Jack exercised before lunch was a newly cut and badly-behaved ex-stallion.

The animal should have been gelded at six months. But his owners had harbored breeding aspirations until he turned three and they realized they weren't capable of managing a stallion. Castrated shortly before being brought to Jack 'to sort out,' the horse still had enormously high testosterone levels.

The big black brute was poorly managed in his early years and Jack suspected his scared owners had hardly handled him at all.

Unoriginally named Macho and used to pushing his humans around, coming to Jack's farm was proving a rude awakening.

Luca and Frank had to combine forces to groom the horse and put on the surcingle and lunging cavesson.

As a rule, Jack preferred not to lead horses with a chain over their nose, but it was a matter of safety with this guy. Luca led him from the left side with the chain lead and Frank led from his right side with a regular lead rope.

Jack was starting this wild horse's training without using a bit. He had to teach submission, but also wanted to demonstrate to the animal that no one was trying to hurt him.

The side reins were long enough for him to stretch his neck down long and low. Nevertheless, there followed many rounds of bucking and galloping in circles, with Jack in the center digging in his heels to prevent being hauled over by this whirlwind.

Macho needed to understand that he could stop working as soon as he gave the trainer a few good circles. When the horse finally lowered his neck and relaxed into a rhythmic trot on both reins, he was asked to halt. The exhausted animal stood with his head lowered as Jack walked up to give his nose a rub and scratch his withers in reward.

Luca and Frank came and unbuckled the side reins.

"Macho man, just behave and you won't need to work so hard," Jack told the new gelding.

He was quiet enough for Luca to lead back alone to the barn, using the regular lead rope without attaching the chain. Frank walked on the other flank, just in case, but Jack was confident that with regular work the horse would soon quieten down. Being late cut, the animal would retain the intelligence of a stallion even after his male hormone levels decreased. He would never be an amateur ride, but in capable hands he could become a successful competition horse. He had three good gaits and a show jumper's build. Jack looked forward to seeing what he could do over fences.

The two boys jumped down from the bleachers with their dogs in tow, and Joe asked, "Is it time to go to the cabin yet?"

The trainer laughed good-humoredly. Like himself, that kid was always hungry. "Yes, it is. Let's go help Felicia get the food into my truck."

Mrs. Ross was coming down the metal steps of the bleachers and Jack held out his hand to help her off the last one.

I never did this for Jill...

"Thank you, Mr. Harper." She pointed towards the excited youngsters and dogs running into the farm house. "You'd think they'd never been on a picnic before."

"I suspect it's pretty rare for Joe to go on one, isn't it?"

"Yes, unfortunately. Picnics are a challenge for him and it's great to know he'll be able to eat everything you provide, for a change."

Jack obeyed a sudden urge to touch his hat. "I'm glad my condition is of use to him."

Her blue eyes widened anxiously. "I do hope you don't think I'm making light of it."

"Nope, that remark was sincere. It's been a privilege to help Joe."

"You've been invaluable to him, Mr. Harper."

He and Mrs. Ross had reached the front porch steps and Jack was about to tell her to call him by his first name, when the familiar battered blue sedan pulled up by the house.

Jack stifled a sigh. "I don't think you've met our parish priest."

The black-robed figure exited his vehicle. "Ah, Jack! I thought I'd come by and see how my dog is doing."

"You have a dog, Father?" Mrs. Ross asked, walking towards the clergyman, hand extended. "Good morning, I'm Laura Ross."

So that's her first name!

"Hello, Laura! Pleased to meet you."

The priest gets to call her by her first name, but I don't!

The pastor continued, "I'm Father Michael and yes, I do have a dog, but he lives here." He looked at this lady, trying to place her, without success.

"Mrs. Ross is Joe's mother," Jack explained. "He's here for a visit, and will be very happy to see you."

"How perfectly splendid!"

"Mr. Harper, do you mind calling me Laura?" Joe's mother suddenly said. "Mrs. Ross sounds so formal."

Finally!

"If you call me Jack."

He ignored the priest's odd look at this exchange.

He saw Laura notice it, too, and she said hurriedly, "So why does your dog live here?"

Jack intervened. "It's a rather long story. We'll fill you in on the way to our picnic."

Felicia emerged from the house with Joe and Robert, all three of them bearing baskets of food. Katie and 'Flex trotted behind, noses in the air, catching the odors of roast chicken, pork and beef wafting from the containers.

"Father Michael!"

"Hello, Joe! You're looking very hale and hearty. Still riding that big pony of yours?"

"You bet, Father! Are you coming with us? We're having a picnic down at Mr. Jack's cabin."

Jack quickly invited him. "You'll be able to play with your dog as well," he added sarcastically.

What's the real reason he's here?

"Hi, Father. Have you come to see 'Flex?" Robert asked.

He winked. "Yes, I thought I should pay him a visit and make sure you're looking after him properly." Then he pointed to the trunk of his car. "Actually, I came to bring him a couple of bags of dog food."

So, the pastor's unannounced appearance was *not* to check on Jack's evangelical progress. The man was simply fulfilling his duties as a dog owner.

Felicia greeted the priest warmly, pleased he was joining the group.

The horse trainer brought his truck round. "Adults go in the cab, youths and dogs in the back." He opened the tailgate and pulled down the extra step.

Robert and Joe whooped happily and placed the food baskets in the bed of the truck.

"How far is it?" Joe's mother asked nervously.

"It's a seven-minute drive." He realized he'd blithely taken over the parental role with Joe's parent standing right there. "I'm sorry, I should have asked your permission first for him to go in the back. I promise to drive slowly."

"Mom! Don't say I can't!"

Laura ran a nervous hand through her black curls. "I guess it's O.K."

She's used to worrying about her son all the time.

"We'll be fine, Mom — we have the dogs to hold onto!"

"Right, like *they're* going to help." She gave him a scathing look. "Go on, then."

"Thanks, Mom! C'mon Katie, hup!"

"C'mon 'Flex, hup!" Robert echoed.

The two pushed each other jovially out of the way in their haste to get into the bed of the pick-up with their excitedly panting dogs.

Meanwhile, Jack noticed Father Michael discreetly open the back door of the vehicle and fold his soutane underneath him as he slid onto the worn seat. He closed the door and wound down the old-fashioned window for air.

Sly old fox! Jack thought and opened the front passenger door for Laura.

Once in the driver's seat, he turned the key in the ignition and put the truck in gear, aware of Laura next to him and Father Michael's beady eyes meeting his in the rear-view mirror.

He rolled down his window and shouted back to the boys, "Hang on guys! We're leaving!" then looked over at Laura. "Truly, don't worry about them. Like I promised, I'll drive slowly and they won't come to any harm."

She shook her head in self-deprecation. "I know, I know, I try too hard to protect him, and he doesn't need it."

"He really doesn't. He's very self-disciplined and can take care of himself, now."

"And he's bulked up a lot since I last saw him," Father noted.

"That's from working out at the gym every day," Laura said. "He doesn't want to look like a sick kid."

"He certainly doesn't look like one!" Father replied, then added, "Look at Jack here. You'd never know to look at him that he has the same condition."

Jack was beginning to suspect the priest of having an agenda and wished he'd back off.

Laura agreed with Father. "It's wonderful to see what a normal life you lead, Mr. – I mean, Jack. It gives me so much hope for Joe."

Jack didn't know how to respond. Instead he said, "In just a few more minutes you'll see the lake."

The back fields of his property were giving way to dense woodland and the descending track became rutted. Aware of the youngsters in the bed of his truck, Jack slowed down more.

"Thank you," Laura said.

Robert shouted, "Hey, look at that!"

Jack leaned out of the truck. "What d'you see?"

"There's a huge stag in the woods. He must have at least sixteen points!"

"You got your cell phone out?"

"Yup!"

"Can you still see it?"

"Yup!"

"Get ready, I'll stop so you can take a shot. Stopping *now*."

Laura leaned towards Jack in her efforts to see the deer and his heart rate went up.

The animal was standing about fifty feet away, stock still, hoping the humans couldn't see him. He blended so well into the surrounding woods that Jack wasn't sure Laura could make him out.

Aware of her perfume, he pointed and whispered, "Can you see that light-colored tree? Right next to it, if you look carefully, you'll see what appears to be a – "

"I see him!" she breathed excitedly. "He's beautiful!"

Jack leaned farther out of the window and twisted back to ask in a lowered voice, "Get your shot, Robert?"

The youngster breathed the words, "Wait a second, Mr. Jack. There! Got him!"

"Well done! O.K. hang on, we're off!"

Laura sat upright in her seat again, giving Jack back his space. Again, he caught sight of Father Michael in the rear mirror.

"Did you see him, Father?"

"Oh, yes! I saw all right."

Jack's eyes narrowed.

What was that supposed to mean?

He cleared his throat. "Then let's roll."

The pick-up bumped over the rough terrain for a couple more minutes before the trees gave way to a large clearing which sloped gently down to the lake.

The glistening expanse stirred even Jack, who'd seen it countless times.

"This is a lovely spot," Father said. "And what a perfect cabin!"

The log structure was set back a hundred feet from the water's edge to their right, affording a perfect view over the lake.

Jack glimpsed surreptitiously at Laura. She said nothing, but her eyes were wide with wonder and a half-smile lingered on her face. He was glad she was impressed.

Why did I never bring Jill down here?

At the rustle of activity in the truck bed he shouted, "Not yet, guys! Let me park first."

Laura had recovered enough to say, "Jack, this is stunning! I bet you come down here often to get away from it all."

Recalling the nights spent here to escape from Jill, he smiled ruefully. "Yep, I do." He parked behind the cabin so his old vehicle wouldn't ruin the vista. "O.K. boys, you can disembark now."

"Does that go for me, too?" the priest asked.

Jack turned to him. "If you promise to behave."

He was aware of Laura's shocked look, but Father Michael understood his meaning.

The priest grinned. "Scout's honor, Jack." He opened his door and said innocently, "Now, where's my dog?"

Robert and Joe were already carrying the baskets to a rustic wooden table on the patio in front of the cabin, followed by their faithful canines.

Once they'd deposited the containers, Joe said to Robert, "Let's throw sticks for the dogs!"

Jack saw Laura shaking her head. He sensed she was about to ask her son to help with the food, and stepped towards her. "If *you* don't mind, *I* don't mind. It's good to see them having fun. And Robert is in dire need of a friend his own age."

"Why, what's wrong?"

"He's suffered badly from bullying at school," Father Michael said. "Jack's working his magic on him and turning him into a confident person."

Jack's cheeks were burning. He alternated between wanting to thump the pastor and gratitude for painting him in such a good light.

"Then Joe isn't the only teen you've turned around?" Laura said.

The priest spared Jack the need to reply. "He thinks he has no talents beyond training horses, but you and I know better."

"Do we ever!"

To hide his growing embarrassment Jack walked over to the table. "Shall we unpack the picnic?"

Fifteen minutes later the three adults and two teens were seated round the table, while two very wet dogs lay on the ground panting, with eyes raised towards the boys, hoping some scraps would fall their way.

Father said grace, and Jack noticed that Robert added his 'Amen' to the others'.

Conversation over the meal was lively. Robert talked about his work at the shelter and the story behind his decision to adopt 'Flex, with Father Michael making sure his part in the process was duly documented.

Not to be outdone by the priest, Jack included his own actions, and the three of them vied for prominence in the eyes of Joe and his mother.

Joe then boasted about how he was doing with Duke, remarking that he would love to bring his horse back to Jack's farm and show him how the two of them had progressed.

At this his mother said, "Joe, you can't go inviting yourself to other people's homes. Don't you think once was enough for Mr. Harper?"

Is she simply being polite or hinting that she doesn't want to come back? Jack wondered.

Partly in jest and to let Laura know that she wasn't obliged to come with her son if she didn't care to, he asked Joe, "Can you tow the trailer yet?"

"You *know* I can't! I'll have to ask my Uncle Rob to do it."

"Well, as far as I'm concerned, you and Duke are welcome here any time." Then he added, "I hope you know that your *whole* family is most welcome to visit."

Jack prayed it was a good sign that Laura was staring at her plate.

When the meal was over, Joe said, "Let's take the dogs for a walk, Robert. Katie knows this place really well, and I want to explore."

"And I must get back to writing my sermon for this evening's vigil Mass," Father Michael stated.

"I'll drive you back to your car," Jack said. "Are you O.K. to stay with the boys, Laura?"

She nodded, but the priest insisted, "No, no! It's a fabulous day and I'd love to take a stroll through your woods. I think I saw a little path up the hill leading back to the main house?"

"Yes, it's a much shorter route than the track we drove along. Are you sure you want to walk, Father? It won't take any time at all to drive you."

"I'm serious. I shall embrace this rare opportunity to enjoy Nature!"

"In that case, I'll accompany you to the path."

He and the cleric made their way round the back of the cabin. Behind the parked truck the clearing turned into woodland and the start of a distinct trail through the trees.

"Here's the path, Father. You should reach the house in a few minutes."

"Thank you, Jack. And thank you for a most enjoyable meal. Where should I leave the dog food?"

"On a porch chair, if you would. I appreciate your bringing it."

"You're welcome." He put a hand on Jack's arm. "By the way, you're doing a great job with Robert."

"He's a good kid and a really useful addition to my crew. He makes the day go faster and more smoothly."

"Just being a member of your team has increased his self-confidence. God bless you for taking him on, Jack."

"How about God bless me for getting you a dog?" Jack countered.

"Thank you, Jack." Father Michael looked heavenwards, "and thank you, Lord, for 'my' dog." He punctuated 'my' with air quotation marks.

Jack couldn't resist saying, "See what good things come from helping people, Father?"

"Very funny, Jack. I've also been observing what good things are coming out of *your* helping people."

"I don't know what you mean."

"Oh, yes you do. Good bye! See you at Mass tomorrow!"

Jack watched the dark clad figure stroll along the dirt path and disappear around a bend among the trees. He made a wry face: life was getting complicated and he wasn't sure what to do about it.

Laura was sitting by herself at the table, which had been cleared of food and plates. The boys were running up and down the shore, throwing sticks for the dogs and vanishing into the woods to find more.

He saw her before she saw him. The early afternoon sun shone on her dark hair and lit up her face. Her expression was content as she gazed fondly at her happy son.

Across from the noisy dogs and humans, the resident grey heron sat on a tree stump sticking out of the water. Jack admired its long beak, raised disdainfully above a gracefully curved neck.

This place never failed to exert a quiet charm. For Jack, there was extra magic because Joe was here having such a wonderful time with Robert and the dogs after his long battle with ulcerative colitis.

And then there was Laura. He didn't know how to process his new emotions and it didn't help that she was a recent widow.

She turned her head. "Ah, there you are! Did you give Father a good send off?"

"Yup. And I see you very kindly cleaned up our picnic. Thank you." He took a seat and joined her in watching the boys as they churned up the lake's surface with sticks and chasing dogs.

A profound peace entered his soul.

Laura said, "It's the least I could do. You've been very generous in letting us intrude on your time."

"I don't see it as an intrusion. I'm always happy to see Joe. It's not every day that I get to spend time with a fellow UC sufferer."

"You'd never think that either of you had it, to look at you. I'm so grateful that God brought the two of you together, even though it's hard to see why He would give either of you this horrible disease. Meeting you has been a real blessing for my son."

And for you, too, I hope!

Leaving the thought unspoken, Jack said, "I understand Joe's symptoms came on when his father died. His death must have been very hard on you both."

Laura's eyelids squeezed shut to prevent oncoming tears.

"I'm sorry. I shouldn't have brought it up." Would he ever get it right?

"Please don't apologize. After two years you'd think I'd be used to it. But you can understand why I'm so happy that Joe's life is beginning to go back to a kind of normal." She looked fully at him. "And I have you to thank for that."

Her bright smile under sorrowful eyes made Jack want to hug her and tell her all would be well in the end. Instead he said, "It's a privilege to help him – and you."

Blushing slightly, Laura turned her attention back to the boys. "This is a really tricky topic, Jack, and I hope you don't mind my asking you about it." She swallowed. "My big worry now is, how will this affect Joe when he starts dating? I mean, does he tell every girl he goes out with about his condition? He'll have to be careful what he eats when they do the 'dinner and a movie' thing, won't he?"

Jack was elated that she was confiding in him. "My advice is to let the girl know straight away about his UC so she's aware of what awaits her if she continues to date him. Because she'll need to make long term lifestyle changes if they get serious."

"I imagine you've learned that from experience?" There was sympathy in her blue eyes.

Jack nodded.

"Is that why you're still single?"

Taken aback, Jack felt his face flush. "I've not given it much thought, to be honest. But I imagine that's partly why."

"I'm intrigued! Why 'partly'?"

Jack studiously admired the grey heron which still hadn't moved. "Because I thought I'd done something – and I had *intended* to do it – then it turned out not to have happened at all."

"You're being very mysterious!"

"I'm not trying to be. I've just got a lot of stuff going on right now – things I need to work out."

"Forgive me, I don't mean to pry."

Before Jack could answer, Joe and Robert came running up with the two sodden dogs. "C'mon, Mom!" her son said, "come and throw sticks with us!"

Robert asked, "Mr. Jack, would you come down with us, too?"

The horse trainer rose from his chair. "Sure! And I bet I can throw my stick a lot farther than all of yours put together!"

The four of them ran down to the water where he put his theory to the test.

An hour later the wet dogs and two tired teens were sitting in the bed of the truck while Jack drove back to the house with Laura beside him in the cab.

They sat in comfortable silence until Jack thought about Jill and felt uncomfortable again. Was it wrong to be attracted to Laura so soon after his ex-girlfriend's departure?

The only thing he and Jill had in common was a son who was no longer in their lives and didn't need either of them. They had no other basis for a relationship. And he'd been completely honest with her that it was over between them.

He had known Laura for a mere day and a half and already felt more for her that he ever had for Jill. It was weird and unsettling.

Surely part of the attraction was her being one of those rare people who completely understand how to be with someone suffering from ulcerative colitis.

But she was also a widow of only twenty-four months. Even if she were attracted to him (a big 'if'!) he needed to be respectful of that fact. It was far too early to make any kind of advances ...

Laura broke into his reflections. "I know this is a silly question, but I've been wondering why your Golden Retriever is called 'Katie'? 'Flex has his name for a specific reason, so I was curious about the significance of Katie."

"I've never thought about it."

"Perhaps you know a Katie or a Catherine who means a lot to you?"

Of course! Katie was a shortened form of Catherine. Why had he never realized it?

He blinked. "I never appreciated the connection, but my mother's name was Catherine. I guess that's why I came up with 'Katie.'"

"Ah, that explains it! But you say 'was' – is she not still living?"

"She died a couple of months ago."

"Oh, I *am* sorry. I didn't mean to bring up such a sad topic."

"Don't feel bad. You weren't to know."

"Well, since I've already put my foot in it, I may as well ask: is your father still alive?"

As Jack replied in the affirmative, he suddenly realized that he still hadn't told Joseph Harper the good news about his grandson not being aborted.

He blurted out, "Laura, you're a Godsend. Thank you! You've reminded me of something I should have told my father several days ago, but it completely slipped my mind."

She didn't seem to mind being called a Godsend – in fact he was sure he saw a pleased smile raising the corners of her mouth.

Chapter Fifteen: Two Phone Calls

The next day was Sunday and to Joe's surprise Jack announced he was driving him and his mother to Mass.

"We can go with Felicia and Luca," Joe offered. "What are you going to do for an hour while we're in church?"

"Actually, Joe, I'm coming in with you. I've returned to the faith."

"That's awesome!"

"I think so, too."

Jack could see Laura was dying to know what had led to this, but good manners prevented her from asking. He was glad, since the story hardly put him in a good light.

When the two boys and their two dogs had retired for the night to the room with twin beds, Robert had mumbled something about going to Mass with his parents later that Sunday afternoon.

He slept in while Joe got up to go to Mass with the others. Felicia would be in the house during their absence at church.

He sat in the pew with Laura on one side and Joe on the other, like a regular family. Mother and son may be returning to Virginia this evening, but Jack thanked God for this one hour of companionship with them in His Presence.

Going up to Communion with Laura and Joe was very special to him. He would remember this weekend for a long time.

Back at the farm they were joined by Robert and breakfasted on coconut flour pancakes with maple syrup, and the fried gluten-free pasta, bacon and zucchini that Joe had enjoyed so much the previous morning. Afterwards the youngster tucked into the chocolate chip bread.

"I'll put some in a container for your trip home," Jack offered.

"I wish I didn't have to go."

"Me, too," Robert said.

"And I hate to see you go as well, son. Maybe you can come again soon?" This was directed mainly at Laura whose permission would be needed. But he fervently hoped she would want to come, too.

"Mom? What about it?"

Mrs. Ross was confronted with two pairs of pleading teenagers' eyes. "If Mr. Harper is happy to see you, I'm not going to stop you."

"Like I said yesterday," Jack said, "I'm happy to see the whole family, including Duke, anytime you want to come over." He tried to catch Laura's eye, but she was concentrating on her food.

I wish you wouldn't go...

Mrs. Riceman came to fetch Robert and soon it was departure time for Joe and Laura Ross, too.

The goodbye hug Joe gave Jack exuded confidence and strength. What a contrast to the skinny boy who'd arrived that first time with bad acne, in the middle of a horrible flare and with a horse that terrified him!

Jack hated to see him go, not only because he was genuinely fond of the sixteen-year-old, but also because his mother was leaving.

Laura took his extended hand and put her other one over it. "Thank you, Jack, from the bottom of my heart."

"You're very welcome. I hope you come back before long."

Her answer was a whimsical smile. "Come on, Joe, we must be going. Mr. Harper has things to do."

No, I don't!

Kneeling, Joe hugged Katie tightly. "See you soon, girl! C'm'ere, 'Flex!" He put his arms around the black dog. "See you soon, too!"

Reluctantly he rose and slid into the passenger seat of the black Expedition.

Laura rolled down her window. "Good bye, Jack, and thank you again for a wonderful weekend!"

Joe leaned across his mother. "Bye, Mr. Jack! See you *very* soon!" he yelled.

Jack tried to say 'good bye,' but only managed a grunt, and quickly grabbed the two dogs' collars as they threatened to run after the vehicle.

"I feel the same way, guys."

He waited until the SUV exited the electronic gates before releasing his hold on them.

It wasn't strictly true that he had nothing to do, for he did have one important duty to perform.

Shaking off his sadness, he strode purposefully onto the porch, sat down and pulled his cell phone from its holster. It was 11:30 a.m. – 4:30 p.m. in the United Kingdom and a good time to call his father.

"Hello? Joseph Harper here."

"Dad, it's me."

"Jack?"

"Yes, Dad. How are you doing?"

"Just fine, son. Good to hear from you. Is everything alright over there?"

"Yes. Don't worry, I'm calling with good news."

"I can always do with some."

Jack proceeded to tell his father about Jill's visit and the discovery that his ex-girlfriend hadn't terminated her pregnancy.

Before Jack could explain further, his father stammered, "That's just wonderful! Did Jill bring him over with her? I've been praying and praying about this!"

This comment reminded Jack that he had not yet told his father about returning to the faith. There was a lot he'd selfishly kept from him.

Joseph Harper was overjoyed at the news of his son's return to the fold yet sad to hear that his grandson's whereabouts were unknown.

"I wish I knew, too, Dad and I'm sorry. But at least I don't have his blood on my hands."

"Yes, son, you're right. That *is* the main thing. And we can both thank Jill for keeping your baby instead of the alternative."

On impulse, Jack asked, "How would you feel about coming over for a visit?"

"Do you mean that, son?"

"Yes, I do, Dad." And he actually *did*.

"That would be marvelous. The weather here has been horrendous – I could use some sunshine."

His son laughed. "We've certainly got plenty of that out here!"

They agreed that Mr. Harper would book a flight as soon as possible.

"I look forward to it. Good bye, Dad."

"Good bye, son. And thank you, you've made my day – no, my year!"

Jack ended the call with the fulfilling sensation of having done something good. He should have given his father this news much sooner, but probably wouldn't have invited him over had he not been feeling so empty over the departure of Joe and Laura.

God's timing is always perfect.

As he walked into the house, with the two dogs trotting behind, the cell rang in his holster.

He had to answer: it might be a client, even though they were supposed to call Maggie, his long-time secretary. "Hello?"

Too late, he saw it was Jill's number. He could have kicked himself.

"Hello, Jack?"

He faked enthusiasm. "Hi, Jill! I take it you got back to the U.K. alright?"

"Yes, thanks. My dog was happy to see me."

Was that her way of accusing Jack of *not* being happy to see her? You never knew with women….

"Oh, that's right, Molly, your Old English Sheepdog."

Why is she phoning?

"Yes, well remembered!"

"Is everything O.K. over there?"

Can we keep this short?

There was a pause. "Jack, is there someone else?"

He pretended not to understand. "What do you mean?"

Her voice became petulant. "You know perfectly well what I mean. Are you seeing another woman?"

Jack was tempted to say 'What *other* woman? There was no *original* woman!' but kept it civil. "No, Jill, I'm not."

"Because I got the distinct impression that there must be when I was over there."

It was none of her business. But he truthfully told her, "No, there wasn't anyone when you were here."

"Oh, so there *is* someone now?"

This was getting annoying. "It doesn't matter whether there is, as you say, someone else. The point is that you and I are no longer together. It's over, Jill."

She sighed. "O.K. Jack, I suppose I have to accept that."

Yes, lady, you do!

He said, "It would make your life a lot easier if you *could* accept it and move on."

"Sounds as if *you've* moved on."

He tried to be diplomatic. "We both have to."

"Can we still be friends, though, for the sake of old times?"

"Of course, Jill."

Whatever 'being friends' means.

"O.K. Good bye, Jack."

"Good bye, Jill, take care." He pressed the red button quickly in case she thought of anything else to say.

Sitting at his kitchen table, with two hopeful dogs staring at his chocolate chip bread, Jack thought, *Glad that's over!*

Yet at the same time he continued to feel guilty about his attraction to 'another woman,' as Jill would have put it, so soon after his ex-girlfriend had left.

He found himself thinking about Laura a great deal throughout the next week.

There were a lot of questions on his mind. Was she seeing anyone else? Would she even be interested in a relationship with him? Even if she were, how were they going to manage with her working in Richmond and his business here in Maryland?

Jack hadn't been interested in dating for so long that he wasn't sure how to go about it anymore. The great thing was that Laura already knew he had ulcerative colitis, so he didn't have *that* hurdle to clear.

A couple of days after their conversation, Joseph Harper called to say he'd booked a flight arriving in BWI from Heathrow the next Monday at 7:44 p.m.

Jack was pleased with this choice of airport: he wouldn't have to deal with the heavy traffic to Dulles Airport and BWI was only 45 minutes away from his farm.

With his father's imminent visit to prepare for, his full horse training schedule and Robert to keep an eye on six days a week, Jack kept busy. Only in the evenings did he have the luxury of pondering his next move with Laura – or whether he should even make one.

Robert was rapidly becoming indispensable and Jack wondered how his crew would cope after he returned to school at the end of August.

Obviously, they'd managed before he arrived. But he was so good at getting the horses ready and taking care of them after they'd been exercised that the three men were now accustomed to finishing their work days early. Life without Robert would be a big adjustment.

The kid had grown so confident. Jack felt bad about taking money off his parents for this time, but that had been the deal.

Plus, he'd ended up with a second dog. Was Father Michael really looking for another family to take care of 'Flex when Robert went back to school? And did he mean what he'd said about keeping the dog at his place if he hadn't found that new home?

He then recalled the verse from Matthew's Gospel about today's trouble being sufficient for today[4]. August was still two weeks away, so why concern himself with it now?

He had no control over tomorrow.

Leave it in God's hands, Jack.

However, Robert was less cheerful than usual. On the Wednesday after Joe left, Jack finally asked him if anything was wrong?

The kid looked embarrassed. "Not really wrong, Mr. Jack. It's just that – "

"Just that what?"

"Well, it was a lot of fun having Joe here." He looked sideways at the trainer. "Is there any way he could come back again? You know, like you said he could – and I'd love to see his horse, Duke."

"We did have a good time, didn't we?" Jack paused a moment. "I tell you what, why don't I give you Joe's phone number? You can ask him if he'd like to come back with Duke to show us how they're doing."

"I already have his number. We've been texting every day – he really wants to come back!"

This was music to Jack's ears. "Then he needs to check with his mother."

How do I make sure she comes with him?

"Tell Joe to ask his mum back, too. I don't want her to feel left out. Joe's uncle will have to haul Duke here and Mrs. Ross may think she's not invited as well."

Robert's face beamed. "Awesome! I'll get on it right away! How soon can they come?"

"As soon as they like."

The sooner the better!

---

[4] Matthew 6:34

Chapter Sixteen: Joseph Harper

Immediately after saying it, Jack realized he needed to modify that statement.

His father was coming on Monday and his son ought to spend at least a couple of days with him before more company joined them.

"Robert, we'd better make that any time after Tuesday. My dad might feel a little put out if he has to deal with a houseful of strangers straight away." Jack wondered how to put this: "He's not used to having a lot of people around whom he doesn't know."

"O.K. I'll tell Joe."

*

Sunday came and Jack sat in his pew at Our Lady of Sorrows remembering how good it felt to have Joe and Laura next to him the previous week.

Dear Lord,

I'm sorry to keep asking favors of you, but please let me know if it's O.K. to have feelings for Laura?

I don't want to do the wrong thing, and after every wrong thing I've already done, I don't deserve to be happy. But forgive me for asking you anyway.

Oh, and my father is coming tomorrow. Please could you make sure we get on and that he has a good time?

Thank you.

Amen.

After riding on Monday, Jack had time to take a quick shower and grab a bite to eat before driving to BWI to meet his father's flight.

It was almost 10 p.m. by the time Joseph Harper completed the grueling customs and immigration process and rolled his suitcase through to his waiting son.

They hugged each other affectionately: his father was still thin but in good spirits.

The drive back to his farm was not nearly as stilted as their time in the car a short two months ago, when Jack returned to England for his mother's funeral.

That ninety-minute drive from Heathrow airport along the M4 to the West Country had been excruciating. With no mutual interests they'd been forced to stick to mundane topics.

But this time it was different. Mr. Harper senior asked for more details about his son's return to the Church and Jack was happy to oblige.

He talked about Joe's uncle asking him to take on his nephew and the kid's horse: how learning about Joe's ulcerative colitis persuaded him to help the teenager despite his aversion to working with kids.

He enjoyed telling the story, reliving the experience of showing the teenager how to overcome his disease, while he and Duke regained trust in each other so Joe could ride him with other horses in the warm up arena again.

"Sounds as if you really have a way with kids, son."

"And you sound like Father Michael, Dad."

"Who's Father Michael?"

"The priest who brought me back into the Church. He also talked me into taking on another kid, which led to my having a second dog on my property."

"You *have* been busy since I last saw you!"

By the time they reached the electronic gates of Jack's property, the two of them had just about caught up on their news. But there was one last thing Jack needed to tell his father. As they sat in his sitting room enjoying a late-night snifter, Jack broke the news that they would have more visitors in two days.

Mr. Harper didn't look pleased, but was more amenable to the idea when Jack explained who they were. "At least I have tomorrow alone with you."

Jack knew this wasn't entirely true, as he would be fetching Robert from the dog shelter at noon and bringing him back for lunch before the two of them went to work in the afternoon. But he decided to tell this to his father in the morning.

As they parted for the night, Joseph Harper placed his hand on Jack's shoulder. "It's really good to see you again, son."

"Same here, Dad. Sleep well."

*

Jack woke up in the morning with a plan to cheer his father up after breaking the news about Robert's being a daytime fixture on the farm.

"Welcome back, señor!" Felicia cried, giving his father a hug and plying him with food. Mr. Harper had last visited five years ago with his wife.

"I keep forgetting about your interesting diet, Jack."

"Keeps me out of trouble – and it's good for you, too, Dad."

"If you say so! What are your plans for today?"

"I thought we might go on a gentle trail ride this morning. What do you say? You remember Papa, don't you?"

"I certainly do. He's a nice quiet horse."

That settled, Jack added, "You recall that I talked about Robert, another kid I'm kind of mentoring? He doesn't sleep at the farm, but he comes every day to help with the horses and spends Tuesday and Friday mornings at the local dog shelter."

"So that's where he is this morning?"

"Yes. I pick him up at noon. He'll have lunch with us then help me with the horses this afternoon. When he goes home, we'll have the rest of the evening to ourselves before Joe and his horse arrive tomorrow."

"It all sounds very complicated, but I'll try and 'go with the flow' as they say."

"They're good people, Dad. It'll be fine."

Fingers crossed.

After breakfast Mr. Joseph Harper got back on Papa after a five-year break, with help from his son, who rode the old show jumper, Bentley.

"Mind if we bring the dogs, Dad? They enjoy trail rides."

"As long as they don't spook my horse!"

"Papa is pretty spook-proof."

They took the trail through the woods down to the cabin, with Katie and 'Flex running in front, racing each other. The sun filtered through the interwoven leaves overhead as father and son made their way along the dirt path through the trees.

The land began to slope downhill. "Lean back a little, Dad, to make it easier on Papa."

"Like this?"

"Yup, that's good."

After a while they entered the clearing by the cabin. The two dogs were already splashing around in the lake and Jack said, "Follow me," as he walked Bentley down to the water. The horse took a few steps in then stretched his head down to take a drink.

Papa joined in and a few moments later they waded farther into the lake in a foot of water parallel to the shoreline.

Bentley lowered his head for another drink but Papa pawed at the water with his right foreleg.

Joseph Harper laughed. "He's enjoying this, isn't he?"

"Yes, Dad, but a little too much. He's actually preparing to go down and roll, so you'd better kick him on instead!"

His father energetically urged his horse forward. A surprised Papa broke into a trot and Bentley followed suit, not wanting to be left behind.

When the big animal caught up with the 15 hand paint the two men burst out laughing.

"I actually enjoyed that!" his dad said.

"We can trot some more if you like."

"No, I don't want to push my luck."

"Then we'll head back for home. Do you want to come to the dog shelter with me to pick up Robert? I think he'd like that."

"If you think he would, I'm happy to tag along."

"It's not tagging along, Dad. I want you to be a part of my activities."

His father gave him such a happy smile that a lump rose in Jack's throat. He thought how elated his mother must be that the two of them were getting along.

"You know, Dad, someone recently asked me why I call Katie by that name."

"Oh, what's the answer?"

"I'd never thought about it before, but I'm sure I subconsciously named her after Mum."

"That's great, son. She'd be very pleased."

"I like to think so."

They rode uphill in single file through the woods back to the house, each man deep in his own thoughts, with the tired dogs taking the rear.

As the barn came into view, Jack asked, "Dad, how soon after you met Mum did you know she was the one?"

The answer came without a second's hesitation. "The first moment I set eyes on her, son."

Chapter Seventeen: More Visitors

Jack and his father pulled up outside the dog shelter and Robert jumped into the back of the Evoque with 'Flex. Jack always brought the dog along.

"Hi there, boy!" The kid was in very high spirits, and after introductions were over, Jack asked, "Have a good morning?"

"Yes sir! But tomorrow'll be even better when Joe gets here!"

Jack echoed that sentiment, but it would be unseemly to express it and show more interest in the coming guests than his current overseas one.

"You and Joe get on well, I take it?" Mr. Harper asked.

"Yes sir! We get to play with the dogs down at the cabin with Mr. Jack. And Joe is bringing his horse this time, so I'll get to see him ride, too."

The older man gave Jack a glance that meant: *You used to hate kids!*

His son ignored him.

*

That night Jack got little sleep. This was irritating as his job was very physical and he needed his eight hours. But excitement over Joe and Laura's pending arrival provided him with enough energy the next day to get through six horses before lunch.

However, during the meal it was hard for him to act as a foil to Robert's feverish anticipation. He told his father, "You'd think he hadn't seen Joe for ten years, instead of ten days!"

"He's even making me keen to meet him!"

After lunch they put the food away and placed plates in the dishwasher, while Robert kept checking through the kitchen window for Joe.

Then he shouted excitedly, "I see them! There's a truck and trailer coming up the drive – that's got to be them!"

Jack pretended not to care, trying to control the crazy pumping of his heart. He dared not look at his father – convinced his face would give him away.

"C'mon, 'Flex! C'mon Katie, Joe's back!" Robert ran out onto the porch and waved wildly at the grey truck and tagalong trailer pulling up to the house.

The pick-up had barely come to a stop before Joe tore open the passenger door and rushed over to his friend and the dogs.

Mr. Brady exited more sedately and walked over to Jack, who introduced his father.

"All the way from England, I presume?" Mr. Harper nodded and Joe's uncle continued, "Welcome to the U.S. You must be proud of your son. He's a miracle worker!"

Hoping his father would attribute his red face to embarrassment over this compliment, Jack told Mr. Brady, "That's a gross exaggeration. You are staying with us, too, I hope?"

"Yes, if that's O.K. Mrs. Brady has given me permission." He winked.

"Good. Did Joe's mother come this time?" He'd noticed there was no one else in the vehicle and was trying to hide his disappointment.

"Laura? No, she couldn't get the time off work."

"That's a shame," he said nonchalantly.

Doesn't she want to see me again?

"But she'll be here on Friday. She's going to try and get off early and be here in the late afternoon."

To cover up his elation at this news Jack said, "Shouldn't we get your horse off the trailer, young man?"

"Yessir!" Joe pulled Robert to the front of the transport and pointed proudly at the bay poking his nose out of the side window. "This is Duke!"

*

Over the next two days Jack observed how his father handled the sudden whirlwind of activity amid strangers.

Two young adults, two bouncy dogs and an uncle on the farm were a lot for the quiet man to contend with. But he coped with dignity.

By evening on the first day he was sitting on the porch with Jack and Uncle Rob, who by now were on first name terms. Drink in hand, the three men watched the sky darken over Joe and Robert, who were teaching tricks to the two dogs and vying with each other over whose animal learned the fastest.

Rob Brady was a farmer and Joseph Harper was a retired accountant, but they still found plenty to talk about. And Jack was glad not to be alone with his father just now as there might be awkward questions.

During a break in the dogs' training, Robert said to Joe, "Hey, I just thought. Your uncle has the same name as me!"

Joe grinned. "Uncle Rob, your real name's not Robert, is it?"

"No," his uncle replied. "Believe it or not, my real name is Richard."

"Then why are you called Uncle Rob?"

"My initials are Richard Oliver Brady so I got called 'Rob' at school and it stuck."

"Glad my initials don't spell another name," Robert said.

Jack thought, *Yes, you didn't need any more reasons to get bullied.*

*

Night had descended.

"O.K. boys," said Jack, "time to take you to the cabin."

Robert and Joe had obtained their parents' permission to sleep in the cabin on condition the two dogs were with them.

"Can we sit in the bed of the truck again?" Joe asked.

Jack looked at the teenager's uncle.

He nodded. "You're only young once."

And what stupid mistakes we make!

When the old pick-up drew round, the boys whooped and loaded their suitcases onto the back-passenger seat with the dogs' paraphernalia before hoisting themselves and their canines into the bed of the truck.

"See you shortly," Jack told the two men and drove into the darkness.

*

The next morning the boys walked up to the farm house with Katie and 'Flex and ate a hearty breakfast.

Jack gave Robert the rest of the day off after he'd brought in and fed the horses, and Joe gave his friend a riding lesson on Papa in the indoor arena, while Rob Brady looked on.

Then Joe rode Duke in front of Robert in the outdoor arena, where Jack could watch him while training his clients' horses. The teenager was justly proud of how beautifully in sync he was with his horse.

Mr. Harper spent the morning watching his son from the bleachers and Jack hoped he liked what he saw. His father could be hard to read, but the fact that he remained on the hard metal seat all morning indicated some interest in his son's work.

When the five of them reconvened over lunch Joe remarked on how well Robert had done with his riding lesson and Jack congratulated Joe on his progress with Duke.

Both boys were pleased with their morning.

Quiet up until now, Mr. Harper said, "I must say, Jack, you really know what you're doing with those equines."

"Thanks, Dad, glad you think so."

I wish Laura would get here!

He suggested the boys go down to the cabin with Uncle Rob and Mr. Harper while he rode his afternoon horses.

"You can take the pick-up if you like, Dad. It may be too far for you to walk."

Mr. Harper snorted at the idea. "I'm not in my dotage yet, thank you! I'll take shank's pony with the rest of them. It'll do me good."

The three Americans looked at him in confusion.

Mr. Harper was surprised. "What? Don't you know what shank's pony is?"

They shook their heads.

Jack laughed. "It's an old-fashioned term for walking."

"O.K. let's *all* take shank's pony!" Robert said, and the four humans set off with the two dogs.

*

The next day was Friday. Robert spent the morning at the dog shelter and Joe went fishing down at the lake with his uncle.

Mr. Harper offered to fetch Robert at noon to free his son up to finish his chores early. "Then you'll be done by the time Joe's mother arrives," he added slyly.

His son narrowed his eyes. "That's not necessary, Dad."

"But I do think it's a good idea, don't you? I'll be fine if you draw me a map. It's not that far away as I recall."

Wanting to hug his father, Jack drew the map. "Call me if you get lost. I can be there in a jiffy."

"No need to fuss. I'll be back soon with the boy. But I'd better take your pick-up."

Jack happened to prefer it, too. When had Dad last driven an automatic? When had he ever driven on the other side of the road, for that matter?

Watching his father slowly make his way down the drive Jack threw up a quick prayer.

This extra gift of time was enough for him to lunge Goliath and smarten up before lunch. Laura might arrive soon after the meal and he didn't want to be conspicuous by disappearing in front of everyone immediately after eating to spruce himself up. Rob Brady had no clue about Jack's feelings for his sister, and Jack wanted to keep it that way.

Mr. Harper drove back safely with Robert, and Joe returned from the lake with Uncle Rob. Felicia had prepared a healthy steak salad which everyone ate with gusto as they chatted animatedly about their mornings.

Except Jack, who was frustrated by how long the meal dragged on. Was Laura on the road yet, or had she got stuck late at work?

"You're very quiet, Jack," his father remarked. "Everything O.K.?"

"Sure, Dad," he lied. "I was just letting everyone else talk, that's all." He made an effort to join the conversation.

After lunch the three adults were sitting on the porch drinking coffee or, in Jack's case, iced water, when the electronic gates opened to let in the black Expedition.

"Oh, there's Laura now," her brother casually remarked, looking at his watch. "She made very good time!"

I hope that's because she was anxious to get here.

She pulled up and exited the vehicle. Those deep blue eyes, so candidly greeting his at their first encounter, looked at him fleetingly from a flushed face.

Jack introduced her to his father, whose hand she shook firmly. "I'm so glad to meet you, Mr. Harper. I hope Maryland agrees with you."

"This place is so busy I haven't had time to think about it!"

Laura laughed gently. "We do seem to be crowding your son, I'm afraid."

"Oh, I don't dislike the company, Mrs. Ross. It's very refreshing after my quiet English routine."

Jack stifled a laugh. *Dad <u>hates</u> company. He's just as smitten as I am!*

Rob Brady gave her a hug. "Hi sis! Good drive up?"

"Easy. I couldn't believe my luck with the traffic."

"Surprised that old SUV of yours in still running."

"It's in better shape than *your* ancient vehicle!"

Katie and 'Flex trotted up from behind the house with Joe and Robert.

"Hi, Mom!" Laura's son waved.

"Aren't you going to give your mother a hug?" his uncle asked.

Laura answered for him. "We saw each other last weekend, Rob. Sixteen-year-olds are too grown-up to hug their mothers every five minutes!"

"See, Uncle Rob? Mom gets it."

Laura shook her head.

"Can I get your bags?" Jack asked.

"Oh, I didn't bring much. I can get them, thanks. Aren't we keeping you from your horses?"

Is she pushing me away?

"How long are you here for?" Joseph Harper asked.

"I have to go back on Sunday."

"Sorry to hear that," Joseph Harper said, echoing his son's feelings.

"Work beckons, I'm afraid. I wish I could stay longer – like someone I know!" Joe was standing next to her and she ruffled his blond mop.

He ducked out from the unwanted attention, smoothing his rebellious hair while his mother opened the back door of the Expedition and took out a large leather hold-all.

"Sure I can't help you with that?" Jack tried again. He could see it was heavy.

Laura relented with a playful grin. "If you really have the time, I won't say no."

"I do have the time." He took the bag. "Yours is the same room as before, I hope that's O.K."

Joe followed them both into the house, to Jack's relief. It eased the bizarre tension.

That afternoon he had to ride three more horses and envied his father's spending time with Laura and her brother. But when Joe brought Duke out to ride in the arena, his mother sat in the bleachers to watch.

Still on duty, Robert took Rolando from Jack, who'd finished working with the horse and walked into the middle of the arena to teach Joe.

It was clear the teenager had been working on Third Level movements from the horse's more collected frame.

"Let's see your trot half-pass."

As Joe obliged, Jack told him "More outside rein! More outside leg – not too much – he's leading with his quarters now – put your inside shoulder back to free up *his* shoulders. Good! Now change rein. This is his more difficult side – get him to step underneath himself more, Joe – use more outside rein…"

Joe followed instructions and Jack enjoyed the improvement in Duke's elevation at the trot and the horse's increased engagement from behind.

I need to find out if he's got a higher level instructor at home. I'm not a dressage expert, and he's going to need someone better than me!

When the lesson was over, Laura stepped down from the metal bleachers, clapping. She looked up at her son on the big horse. "Wow, Joe! You and Duke were dancing!"

"Thanks, Mom!" He beamed. "I told you Mr. Jack was a good instructor."

Jack stood slightly apart from them not wanting to intrude, but Laura turned to him. "I'm not a horse rider, so it all appears magical to me. When you ask Joe to make a small adjustment in the saddle, the changes in the horse are huge."

She was talking about horse training, his favorite subject, and Jack lost self-consciousness. "That's the art of dressage: appearing to do very little while constantly giving subtle cues to the horse. Joe and Duke could go far, if they wanted to."

Joe dismounted and stroked his horse's neck with affection. "I'd love to go up the levels with him."

Laura tilted her head slightly. "And to think that just a few short weeks ago my son wouldn't have entertained the thought!"

The dogs began barking at the sudden arrival of Mrs. Riceman's burgundy Camry. What was up? Robert was supposed to be staying at the ranch during Joe's stay.

She exited her vehicle hurriedly, holding out a large piece of paper. "Hello, Mr. Harper. Hello, Laura, Joe. Is Robert here?"

"He's in the barn, Mrs. Riceman, is anything wrong?" Jack asked.

Joe handed over Duke's reins. "I'll go get him." He ran to the stable building.

She handed Jack the white sheet. "This was shoved under our front door just now."

Jack took it from her and Duke stretched his muzzle hopefully towards it. "No, buddy, this isn't a treat."

The note was laughably crude, written with the stereotypical clipped newspaper letters, and read:

SAY YOUR SORRY OR THE DOG GETS IT!

The poor grammar added humor to the note, but the situation wasn't funny. Someone was out to get 'Flex and Jack had a good idea who.

Robert came running out of the barn. "What is it, Mom? It's not time for me to go home yet."

Jack showed him the note. "No one's trying to make you go home, Robert. But your mom just got this."

"It's that crazy Max! He never could tell the difference between 'you're' with an apostrophe and 'your.' He's just trying to scare me because my dog protected me from him at the shelter. School will be starting soon, and he's hoping to bully me again." He bent down to stroke his dog's head. "But we're not going to let that happen, are we 'Flex?"

Jack was amazed at the kid's calmness. He really had come a long way.

"Dude, that's a real threat!" Joe said.

"Yes. What if he's serious?" his mother asked.

Jack said, "I'd be surprised if Max really did try to take the dog, Mrs. Riceman. 'Flex doesn't like him and that bully is scared of him. It wouldn't end well for Max if he did make a kidnap attempt."

"I do hope you're right! But don't you think we should take some precautions?"

"Would you feel better if I slept in the cabin with the boys until this is cleared up?"

"Would you, Mr. Harper? That would ease my mind."

"Sure thing. And we'll all keep an eye on 'Flex."

"But *Mom*! We've got the dogs to protect us!"

"That's rather the point, Robert," Jack said. "Someone wants to take away your protection. I don't want to ruin your fun, and it'll only be for a couple of nights. O.K.? Otherwise your mum is going to want you to go home with her."

"I'd *much* prefer to have you home with me, Robert."

Given this choice her son decided that having Jack at the cabin wasn't so bad after all. "O.K. I guess I do need to stay here and protect 'Flex."

"Good decision," said Jack. "I'll just be there for backup."

He could tell Robert's mother still wasn't sure about this arrangement, but didn't want to be rude by saying so. She gave Robert a big hug and an admonition to be careful, then reluctantly got into her car and drove away.

They all walked back onto the porch in somber mood.

Laura said, "Robert, since 'Flex is technically Father Michael's dog, shouldn't we let him know about this?"

Jack wanted to kick himself for not thinking of it, and was glad she had.

"Yes, ma'am." He and Joe went into the house, dogs at their heels, to make the call.

Laura took a seat on the porch swing, and Jack's father sat with Uncle Rob on the sofa. Jack hoped Laura didn't mind his taking the space next to her.

He leaned forward with his elbows on his knees. "We all need to keep an eye on 'Flex." He looked at his hands thoughtfully. "And we probably should pay attention to where Katie is, too. I know Max won't dare to grab 'Flex, so he may take my dog in revenge. If you would all be aware of where they both are, I'd be very grateful."

He twisted to include Laura in this petition. She lifted her hand as if about to place it on his shoulder in sympathy, then thought better of it and ran her fingers through her black hair instead.

"Did you reach Father Michael?" she asked when the boys returned.

"Yes, he said to keep him 'apprised of events,' whatever that means."

The adults laughed and Uncle Rob said, "It means to let him know what happens next, son."

"Oh," Robert said. "Then why didn't he just say that?"

"I think he forgot he was talking to a teenager. I'd take it as a compliment," Laura said.

"Anyone up for a drink?" Jack asked. "I know I am!" Even though it would have to be a weak one, some alcohol would be better than none.

He took their orders and when Felicia came over to make dinner, she found a melancholy group of people on the porch with a variety of beverages in their hands.

"I hope no one die?" she inquired.

Jack filled her in. "We all have to be aware of the dogs' location, Felicia."

Seeing his house keeper reminded him that there were still horse chores to do. Her son and Frank must be wondering where he was. He got up and called Robert.

"I'll come, too," Joe said. "That way the dogs will be together and we can keep an eye on them."

"Plus, one of the horses is yours," Jack added with a wink.

"Yessir, Mr. Jack!" Joe retorted, making an exaggerated dash to the barn with Katie barking behind him.

"Sorry to abandon you like this," Jack said to his guests, "but Felicia will refill your drinks when you need. We'll be back in a while."

Dinner was served on the porch. Two more chairs were pulled out of the kitchen to accommodate the boys around the patio table, dogs lying by their feet. The group felt safe in this setting and the mood became merrier.

At 9 o'clock Jack rose to collect clothes and toiletries for his overnight stay with the boys. As he packed his things, he felt a childish twinge of disappointment at having to leave the house.

He reappeared on the porch, bag in hand. "I'll bring the truck round, boys, then we'll go to the cabin for the night."

Five minutes later Jack told them to get into the cab with the dogs.

"Aw, can't we ride in the back again?"

"Joe," his mother said, "Mr. Harper's not trying to ruin your fun. He's just being cautious, given the circumstances."

Jack flashed Laura a quick smile of appreciation for her support. "While we're at it, let's grab their leashes. We're going to have to lead them out for their bathroom breaks so they don't run off."

He patted his father on the shoulder. "Good night, Dad. Sorry about this. See you in the morning."

"Never a dull moment around here!" Joseph Harper replied jovially, then became serious. "Keep the boys safe, son."

Jack nodded. "Will do." To Laura and her brother, he said, "I hope you both sleep well. We'll join you for breakfast tomorrow." Then he jumped into the driver's seat. "Let's go boys!"

"'Night!" Joe and Robert yelled from the truck as the headlights pierced the night.

Chapter Eighteen: The Anguish

The cabin had two bedrooms, one with a king size bed and the other with twins. Joe and Robert occupied the latter and each had a dog on his cover.

Before retiring to bed, Jack checked all the doors were locked and the dogs were indeed inside with the boys. Satisfied, he knelt to say his evening prayers, recalling his father's words: 'Never a dull moment around here!'

How had his life switched so swiftly from the routine of riding horses all day and sleeping alone in his house, to having a teenager or two, plus their family, and now his father and a second dog on the premises?

More bewildering was how quickly he'd dismissed Jill from his life and embraced the idea of Laura being in it.

He thought about Joseph Harper's other words: 'The first moment I set eyes on her, son.'

Help me find the right path and not do anything to displease You, Lord. I'm still not sure what I should be feeling and doing.

With a guilty pang he remembered that Robert's dog was under threat.

Dear Lord, please let that come to nothing. Robert doesn't need this: he's made such great progress and it would destroy him if 'Flex were stolen.

Please keep all my guests safe.

Amen.

Having handed everything over to God, Jack climbed under the duvet and closed his eyes.

*

They flew open the next morning at 6 a.m. when Robert rushed into his room.

"Wake up, Mr. Jack! The dogs have gone!"

"What?" Groggily he put his feet on the bedroom floor and drew his fingers through his tousled blond hair.

The kid was in tears. "He's taken *both* dogs, Mr. Jack!"

"How is that possible?" Jack's rubbed his eyes and blinked against the bad news. "Everything was locked up last night. No one could get in, Robert. Are you sure they're gone?"

"They're gone, sir, no kidding."

Joe joined his friend. "Mr. Jack, there's a door open."

Jack shook his head in disbelief and threw on his weather proof Barbour jacket and moccasins. "Where?"

Robert and Joe showed him the back door of the cabin. Unlike the front one which opened inwards, this went outwards. Jack's first thought was that one of the dogs had somehow unlocked it and leaned against it until it let them out.

But how? All the doors had double locks. Not even the smartest canine in the world could undo those!

His eyes narrowed with suspicion. "Did either of you let the dogs out last night after I went to bed?"

Robert was looking steadfastly at the ground while Joe had a perplexed expression.

"O.K. Robert, what happened?"

"I – I – I took 'Flex out for a pee. But Katie didn't come too, and I had the leash on him. Honest."

"I believe you, Robert, but did you lock the door again after you came back in?"

"I – I don't recall."

"I think we have our answer then, don't we? Those dogs couldn't have got out if you'd locked the door."

"But I did *close* it!" Robert protested.

"But you've been teaching him tricks. And isn't one of them how to open a door handle?"

Robert looked crestfallen. "But why haven't they come home yet?"

It was a good question, but Jack took the optimistic viewpoint. "I'm sure they'll be back soon. What time did you let him out?"

"About midnight."

"Hmmm. They've been gone for a good six hours. We'll call the local vet, police and dog shelter. Maybe someone has found them and brought them in.

"Let's leave the back door slightly open in case they come back, and put some food and water out for them. We'll go up to the house and tell the others. After breakfast and a powwow, we'll start looking for them, if they haven't turned up by then. But I'll bet you they just went hunting and are tired. They'll be lying down somewhere and come home later today."

I hope I'm right!

Chapter Nineteen: Hunting Dogs

They hurriedly washed and dressed and piled into the truck after leaving food and water in the kitchen and the back door jammed slightly ajar.

"Robert, you'd better phone Father Michael and apprise him of events, and perhaps let your mum know, too?"

"On it," a chastened Robert replied. At least he knew what the phrase meant now.

Jack dropped the boys off at the house and drove to the barn to tell Luca and Frank what had happened.

"You go look for those dogs," Luca said. "We'll be fine here."

"Thank you, guys." Jack drove back to the house. Both his vehicles would be needed for this search.

On hearing the news Laura put her arm around 'Flex's owner. "We'll find him, Robert. Say a prayer to St. Anthony. He's the patron saint of lost things."

Robert's wooden voice replied, "I don't believe in all that stuff, ma'am."

Joe looked at his friend. "*Seriously,* you don't believe in God?"

Robert said defensively. "Not really. What's the big deal?"

"Actually, it's a very big deal, Robert," Jack said gently. "But we'll talk about it another time. For now, will you let your friends pray on your behalf?"

Shrugging his shoulders, the kid replied, "If you think it'll do any good."

"Thank you, Robert," Laura said and looked around the table. "I presume the rest of us are believers?"

Everyone else nodded.

Good for you! Jack thought.

"Then Mr. Harper, would you please lead us in prayer?"

For a split-second Jack thought she meant him and with disappointment realized she was addressing his father.

"I'd be glad to," Joseph Harper replied and with eyes closed, began. "In the name of the Father and of the Son and of the Holy Spirit."

Robert usually made a poor effort at the sign of the cross when they said grace before meals, but now Jack saw him outline a big one, presumably to be on the safe side.

"St. Anthony, please intercede with the Father on our behalf and help us find Katie and 'Flex. We promise to honor you if you do this by giving to charity."

"Amen!" rang a familiar voice from the doorway. "Glad to see you're soliciting help from on high."

No one had heard Father Michael pull up in the driveway, as there were no dogs to bark at his arrival.

"'Morning, Father, Robert doesn't believe in God," Joe blurted out, much to his friend's annoyance.

"I know, son." He walked up to an embarrassed Robert and patted him on the shoulder. "But God will still help him find 'Flex."

"Father – I'm sorry, I've lost your dog!"

"Don't worry son. With all these people praying for you, how can it not turn out well?"

Robert was lost for a reply and Jack pulled up another chair for the pastor. Felicia had already left, and Laura rose from her seat to pour coffee for him.

"Thank you both very much. Now what have we done so far to recover the pooches?"

*

The rest of the day was spent hunting for the dogs. Jack drove his father down to the cabin, where he'd volunteered to wait for them in case they did come back.

Father Michael took it upon himself to visit 'this Max character' and see if he was behind the failure of either dog to come home. Jack thought this a great idea: hopefully a priest showing up on his doorstep would drag the truth out of the bully.

Uncle Rob took Robert in the Evoque to scour the roads adjacent to the property. Jack took Joe and his mother in the truck around the farm. Jack warned Laura that the trip would be very bumpy: wouldn't she prefer to wait at the farm house?

"The dogs may come back and you'd be doing a very useful job," he said unconvincingly.

With that now familiar tilt of her head Laura gave him a scathing look. "I can handle a bumpy road, Jack, and Luca will be here with Frank to let us know if the dogs return."

"Don't say I didn't warn you." Jack opened the front passenger door for her.

"I'm not made of glass, and I won't sue you if I get a bruise or two."

"Thank goodness for that!" Jack snorted. "But what about your son?"

"Oh, he'd *love* some bruises to show off at school!"

Hearing this Joe said, "So I can sit in the bed again, right, Mom?"

The two adults exchanged glances. Laura looked doubtful but said, "If Mr. Jack is O.K. with it, then I am, too."

"Sure thing, Joe. I need to drive slowly anyway, so we can call the dogs and look for them properly."

Jack wished Laura were next to him in the truck under different circumstances. As things were, he felt it inappropriate to strike up any conversation, so the two of them looked out of their respective windows, calling out the dogs' names.

After an hour of fruitless driving around the property, Jack received a call from his father to announce that Katie had come back to the cabin. "She's exhausted, Jack."

"That's great, Dad, but I wonder why 'Flex isn't with her?"

"I'll let you know if he shows up, son."

"Thanks. Talk to you in a bit."

By noon there was still no sign of 'Flex and Jack suggested they meet back at the house to discuss their next move over lunch.

Joe was thrilled to see Katie again, but felt bad for Robert. "Man, I'm sorry we haven't got 'Flex back yet."

"I knew all that God stuff was rubbish," his friend replied.

Father Michael gave a cough. "Just because we haven't found him yet doesn't mean that we won't, young man.

"And I *can* tell you that Max swears he had nothing to do with 'Flex's disappearance. He does, however, admit to creating the note and wanting to scare you. But he said he had no intention of carrying out his threat. So I told him I wouldn't tell the police about it if he promised me that he and his friends wouldn't bully you anymore – or anyone else for that matter."

Robert was impressed. "Way to go, Father! Thank you!" Then he blushed deeply. "Sorry about what I said."

"You're forgiven, young man." He turned to Jack and handed him the crude note. "Just in case Max doesn't keep his word, hang onto this, would you?"

The trainer gave a hollow laugh. "I will, Father."

They ate lunch on the porch, looking out for the missing dog, while trying to carry on a normal conversation.

After their meal it was agreed that Joseph Harper would go back to the cabin and hope 'Flex turned up while the others continued their search.

Except for the priest: he had his 5 p.m. Saturday vigil Mass to prepare for and preside over.

The afternoon passed the same way as the morning, the one difference being that Jack's father didn't call to report the safe return of the second dog. Discouraged, Jack drove to the cabin to fetch him. They locked the back door but left the food and water bowls outside, and met Uncle Rob and Robert at the farm house.

Jack sent Joe and Robert over to help Luca and Frank with the final horse chores. It was better than having them mope around the house, and allowed the adults to discuss their next move.

Before Joe left for the barn he said, "Mom, we can't leave for home until Robert's dog is back. It wouldn't be right."

Laura's blue eyes had a soft look. "We – ell, if Mr. Harper is agreeable, we can leave you here tomorrow and drive back to pick you up when 'Flex is found."

Jack's dad said, "Suits me!"

Laura gave a low laugh. "Well, I'm glad, but I actually meant Jack."

"Oh, of course you did," Joseph Harper said. "I forget there are two Mr. Harpers in this house."

Laura looked questioningly at Mr. Harper junior.

"You know that Joe and *all* his family are welcome to stay as long as they like."

She gave him a grateful look. "I have to go back tomorrow. But thank you for letting Joe stay. How about you, Rob?"

"I need to get back the farm, Joe: your aunt won't be pleased with me if I make her take care of everything by herself any longer than we already agreed. But I can come back to fetch you and Duke at short notice."

"Let's hope 'Flex is found soon, so none of you is inconvenienced," Jack said. "I think that's what Robert would like the most."

"Yes sir – although I'd like you all to stay longer as well!"

Jack rolled his eyes. "Go help Luca and Frank, you two!"

Talking on the porch, the adults decided that Max was clearly not a threat and agreed that since the boys weren't in any danger, they could sleep in the cabin by themselves tonight.

*

When the teens returned for dinner with the lone Retriever, Jack and Laura found themselves working hard to be upbeat about the situation. His father accompanied Jack, the boys and Katie in the truck to the cabin, where Jack collected his overnight things and clothes to bring back to the main house.

After reminding Joe and Robert to lock the doors and *keep* them locked, Jack drove back to the house with his father, who said, "Laura is a really nice lady, isn't she?"

"Yes, Dad, she is."

"And I understand she's widowed."

"Yes, Dad, she is."

"And she's Catholic."

"Yes, Dad, she is."

"Are you going to do something about it?"

Before he told his father, in the nicest possible way, that it was actually none of his business, Jack's phone rang. "Could you get that, Dad? I need both hands to negotiate the path in this dark."

Joseph did as bid. "Hello? ... That's great news! We'll round up the boys and be over. What's the address? ... Jack knows it? ... Oh, good. Be there shortly." To Jack he said, "They've found 'Flex. Mr. Freeman, a neighbor of yours, was on vacation and just came back to find the dog in his swimming pool. It has an old-fashioned ladder and 'Flex can't climb out. He'll have been in there a long time, poor animal."

Jack found a place to turn the truck around. "Dad, call Robert, would you? He's in my phone contacts."

The boys were overjoyed, and at Jack's insistence, jumped onto the back seat of the truck with Katie. "We're going on the highway, guys, I can't let you ride in the bed on public roads.

"Joe, would you call your mum and uncle to let them know? If they want to come over, they can bring the Range Rover. I'll give them the address."

After a short conversation, Joe said, "Mom says that's fine. She and Uncle Rob don't want to cause overcrowding."

Jack felt that familiar twinge of disappointment, but had to agree she was right. There were already going to be four of them at his poor neighbor's.

It was a two-minute drive and when Jack pulled up at the house, he saw Father Michael's dark blue sedan parked outside.

"I guess Mr. Freeman called Father," Robert said. "It's his phone number on 'Flex's collar tag."

Leaving Katie in the truck and the windows half open, Jack and his father exited the vehicle with Joe and Robert and ran to the back of the house.

'Flex was thrashing around in the water with his front paws on the edge of the pool. He was fortunately in the shallow end, but trying in vain to push himself out with his hind legs. Blood in the water where his back paws had become raw were proof of his efforts over many hours, and the dog was clearly exhausted.

"Hang on, boy!" Father Michael was saying as he handed his watch to the neighbor. "Take this, would you?"

The priest jumped into the water, making a huge splash.

The others watched in astonishment as he waded over to the dog. His black soutane filled with water and billowed out behind, hindering his progress.

"Robert!" he called, "come over and help me lift him out."

Jack ran to the pick-up and grabbed his bath towel for wrapping the beleaguered animal in.

"One, two, three – heave!" the pastor shouted and hoisted 'Flex by his hind end over the lip of the pool.

'Flex was shivering miserably, and Jack gave Robert the towel. "Rub him down really hard – he'll have hypothermia."

Father Michael was wading through the water with labored steps towards the old-fashioned ladder.

"Can I give you a hand?" Jack asked.

"That would be kind," said the drenched pastor.

*

An hour later, Joe and Robert were fussing over 'Flex. The dog lay prone on another towel on the vet's metal table. His back paws were covered in bandages, and a needle was inserted under the skin on his front left paw, with a thin tube running to an intravenous drip bag hooked onto a stand next to him.

Meanwhile Father had gone home to change.

He returned just as the vet's assistant was announcing, "He can go home once that bag is empty. He'll need a *lot* of rest, and those paws will take quite a while to heal. I'll go and fetch his medication and explain what he needs and when."

After the lady left Jack said, "Shouldn't you thank Father for rescuing your dog, Robert?"

For the second time that day, the youngster apologized to the priest.

"I'll forgive you again, as long as you admit that God came through for you, *and* you carry out that promise to give alms."

Robert looked exceedingly foolish and replied, "O.K. Father, I give in."

"Was that a 'thank you, God' I heard you say?" the cleric urged.

Robert repeated, "Thank you, God for giving me back my – our – dog." He looked up at the priest, who grinned.

"Yes, alright, *our* dog. But it's still God who brought him back to us."

Robert asked in a weak voice. "What is 'alms' Father?"

While the teenager had the word explained to him and Father suggested a charity to which Robert could donate said alms, the veterinary assistant came back with the papers to release 'Flex into their custody.

"Whose dog is this?" she asked. "Whose name should I put the invoice in?"

"Mine," Father Michael said stoutly.

Chapter Twenty: Departure Time Draws Near

That night the boys shared the bedroom up at the farm house which contained two beds. But Robert slept on the floor wrapped in his duvet next to 'Flex.

The animal lay on a thick dog bed bought by Robert's parents as their contribution to his adoption, a few days after he came home from the shelter.

The next day was Sunday and Jack decided to let the boys sleep in. He would go to the 8 o'clock Mass alone and Joe could go with his uncle and mother to the noon service with Mr. Harper. That way his guests could have a leisurely breakfast whenever they rose.

With 'Flex safely back, there was no more talk of staying on for extra days. Joe, Laura and Uncle Rob were due to leave that afternoon, as originally planned. But Robert's mother had said her son could remain at the farm to care for his dog until there was a significant improvement in the animal's condition.

Jack walked out of the house towards his Evoque, thinking dejectedly about his guests' imminent departure.

Laura's voice called out to him from the porch, "If you're going to Mass, may I come, too?"

His heart was turning stupid somersaults. "Of course!" He turned and waited for her to catch up with him.

"Thanks," she said, "I want to see if Father Michael has dried out after his ordeal in the swimming pool yesterday!"

Jack gave what he hoped was a normal smile. "And I want to persuade him to let me help pay that vet bill."

"That's kind of you. It must be tough, on a priest's salary." She joined him and they walked together towards the vehicle.

He opened the passenger door for her. "I agree. I hope he's going to be reasonable."

He got in and pressed the ignition button. The Evoque's powerful engine sprung into life with British understatement.

"I really like your dad," Laura said, as they drove off. "Does he often come to visit?"

"I'm ashamed to say this is his first trip in five years."

"Oh, do you usually go over to England?"

"Once more, I'm embarrassed to admit that my first visit to my native country in seventeen years was for my mother's funeral two months ago."

Laura looked mortified, which Jack found annoyingly cute. "I'm not choosing good conversation topics, am I?"

"As you've done before, you're choosing smart ones."

"But they make you feel uncomfortable and I don't mean to do that."

"That's O.K." And he meant it.

"How about if you ask the questions?" she suggested.

"Sure! What do you do back in Richmond that prevents you from staying at my place for extra days even when a dog goes missing?"

Her deep blue eyes twinkled. "Interesting phraseology, Jack."

"Uh-huh." He smiled.

"Well, the answer is I'm a CPA with an accounting firm in Richmond. That's a pretty rigid environment. Not much wiggle room for anything beyond real emergencies."

Like the death of a husband...

"I guess a missing dog doesn't count," Jack conceded.

"Unfortunately, not." She stared out of the window. "But that doesn't mean I don't get any vacation days. I just have to plan ahead, that's all."

Was that a hint? Would she like to come back for longer next time?

Let's keep this superficial for now.

His response was bland. "I guess when Joe goes back to school, both of you will only be able to take Thanksgiving and Christmas off. Is Joe going back to live with you when school starts?"

"That's the plan, now that he's got his health back this summer." She turned to him. "Jack, I still can't thank you enough for that." Her eyes were so blue and soft.

Resisting a fierce temptation to put her hand to his lips, he said, "My mother did the same thing for me, so I'm glad I could help Joe."

"Your mother sounds like a good person. You have – had – two great parents. They clearly brought you up well in the faith, too."

"Well, you already know that I wasn't a practicing Catholic when Joe was here."

"Yes. What changed after he left?"

He gave her a brief look, then focused on the road ahead. "A lot of things." He paused. "One of them was Robert."

She'd done it again! Thanks to her questions, Jack clearly understood the part Robert had played in his return to the Church. He absolutely had to evangelize that kid.

"Jack Harper, you are – as I've said before – a very mysterious man."

"And as I've said before, I'm really not. I just have a lot of things to sort out."

"Well, one day I hope to hear the whole story."

"Maybe," he said, being unintentionally mysterious again.

They'd arrived at the parking lot, and Jack found a space close to the church.

He and Laura walked side by side into the building and found the same pew they'd sat in previously with Joe. Laura whispered in his ear as Father Michael came past them up the aisle, "He looks pretty dry to me!" and Jack laughed.

For the next hour he pretended that she wasn't about to leave.

Chapter Twenty-One: Revelations

During the recitation of the Our Father at Mass, the parishioners standing on either side of them held hands and reached out to Jack and Laura.

The last time, their little family of three had stood with hands folded in front of them during the prayer.

Today Jack and Laura held their neighbors' outstretched hands, which left them not holding each other's.

Feeling an absolute ass, Jack realized that Laura was trying not to be forward, and extended his hand towards her with a foolish grin. She took it, and it felt so right.

At the end of the prayer they both gave an involuntary squeeze before letting go.

For the Sign of Peace, he prepared to shake her hand in the normal way. But Laura wasn't having it and gave him a big hug instead.

Like mother, like son! he thought, instinctively returning the strong pressure and pressing his face against hers. Her perfume was so much sweeter than Jill's! Who knew when he'd be able to do this again?

He hoped the same question was going through her mind.

After Mass it was obvious they wouldn't be able to catch Father Michael alone for Jack to offer his help with 'Flex's vet bill. There were too many parishioners in line, and Jack hardly thought the pastor would want it universally known that he had dived into a swimming pool to rescue a dog.

The discussion would have to wait.

On the walk to the Range Rover he'd have loved to hold hands with Laura. But he thought it too presumptuous and settled for tamely opening the vehicle door for her.

Driving back, he felt comfortable enough to say, "I hope you don't mind my bringing it up, but it must be difficult being a single mother."

"I have good days and bad days."

"I imagine Joe is a great comfort to you."

"I don't know what I'd do without him."

"He's not got your dark hair – I guess he favors his father?"

"He actually looks more like you than his father."

How should he respond to such an odd comment?

"I know that sounds strange," she continued, "but we adopted Joe when we were in England and that's why he doesn't look like either of us."

"In England?"

"Yes. My husband was working over there at the time, and since I was born in England, they permitted the adoption."

Jack nearly ran off the road. "Do you know anything about his birth parents? Did you ever meet them?"

"I never met them, but I believe they were both college graduates – from Bath University, I think – and Joe's dad had told his mother to get an abortion. Can you imagine that?"

Jack's vision became blurred and he struggled to steer the Evoque.

"Are you alright?"

"I'm fine," he lied robustly, blinking hard to clear his eyes. "I guess you weren't impressed with the father, then?"

"Well, would you be? The poor mother! And what courage to go through with the pregnancy and birth by herself, after being abandoned so ruthlessly!"

"That was a rotten thing to do," Jack admitted. "But it does sound as if the father was immature and panicking. Perhaps he regrets his actions and has since apologized to the mother?"

"I doubt it!" Laura said. "But I'm very lucky to have his son."

Jack's mind went into a spin: he was Joe's father! Even Laura had said they looked alike.

That was why he felt an affinity to the kid; why Joe had ulcerative colitis which runs in families; why they both had tousled blond hair and a slim build and loved horses and had the same sense of humor …

He took a deep breath, his heart pounding out of control. This was the perfect scenario: Laura and he were connected to the same boy!

But then it hit him.

He couldn't say *anything* to Laura about this. If she discovered who he was she would despise him and probably never speak to him again, let alone visit him with her – their – son.

For a brief moment he contemplated the possibility of pursuing a relationship with her without revealing his true relationship to Joe. But it would be wrong. And how could he entertain such thoughts on the way home from Sunday Mass?

Why, oh, why were the sins of his past rearing their ugly heads again?

Was God testing his faith? Or did this mean he wasn't truly forgiven?

Should he tell Laura the truth and risk losing her and her – *his* – son? Or should he just carry on as before, with no hope of getting close to Joe's adoptive mother?

Laura would not be a single mother forever. Joe would have a new father soon – but not his real one.

In abject misery he tightened his grip on the steering wheel.

Chapter Twenty-Two: Farewell

He swallowed hard and agreed with her about her luck in adopting Joe. But it brought on her inevitable question, "Have you never thought of having kids, Jack?"

He wanted to scream '*I do have one!*' but cracked a joke about getting on better with other people's children.

This elicited a comment from Laura on how well he got on with Joe and he thought his heart would burst. If only he could tell her!

But he was desperate not to be moody: he wanted her to visit again. Hadn't they practically agreed that she would, in that conversation about vacation?

There had to be a solution to this, there *had* to be! He just needed time.

They joined the others for breakfast and Jack made a supreme effort to be normal. But he knew he was failing when Laura said, "We should probably leave now and let you spend time with your father, Jack. We've intruded long enough."

"But your brother and Joe haven't been to Mass yet." Jack was sure his voice sounded whiny.

"You can go to the 5 o'clock in Richmond, can't you guys? If we leave now, we'll be home in plenty of time."

It's already beginning. I've somehow offended her and she's slipping away.

The boys were upset – at least *they* were allowed to show their feelings – but Joe told his friend, looking at Jack, "We'll be back, won't we?"

"I sincerely hope so, son."

Less than an hour later Duke had been loaded into the trailer. Uncle Rob said his goodbyes and Robert and Joe exchanged farewell punches to the shoulder.

Joe hugged Jack and the trainer's eyes welled with tears. "Good bye, son. I hope to see you very soon."

Laura embraced Mr. Harper senior, who was looking confused. She then stood awkwardly in front of Jack.

His heart was breaking but there was nothing he could say. He extended his hand to her, wanting so much to put his arms around her as he had at Mass this morning!

"A hug for my son, but none for me, Jack?"

Jack gave his best grin. "Technically your son hugged *me*."

"Alright, then, be difficult!" She stepped forward and put her arms out.

His heart soaring, Jack responded with a strong grip around her petite shoulders.

She whispered in his ear, "I don't know how, but I've upset you and I'm sorry."

What? Why do you think you've upset me? Can't we talk about this?

She released him and said in a normal voice, "Take care and thank you again."

Dull with grief, Jack stood with his father, Robert and Katie, watching the little cavalcade leave the premises.

The electronic gates shut behind the vehicles and, Retriever in tow, a depressed Robert walked into the house to attend to his wounded dog. An even more depressed Jack tried to rally his spirits for the sake of his father, who was leaving for England the next day.

"Would you like a drink before lunch, Dad?"

"I'd love one, son, thank you."

"Make yourself comfortable. I'll bring it out to the porch."

He traipsed lethargically into the kitchen and opened the fridge door. If only he could get blind drunk!

He pulled out a gluten-free beer for himself and poured his father a gin and tonic. He handed the full tumbler to his parent, who was sitting on the porch sofa, and carried his bottle over to the swing.

Mr. Harper looked around to make sure Robert was out of earshot, before saying, "What's wrong, son?"

It was a relief to tell his father the whole conversation in the Evoque.

"You mean to say that Joe is my grandson?" Mr. Harper almost shouted, then recalled there was a teenager in the house and lowered his voice.

"Yes, Dad. And he's *my son*, too!" He pressed his beer bottle against his temples. "Why did she apologize for upsetting me? She's the one who seemed upset!"

Joseph Harper said softly, "You *were* very taciturn over breakfast, Jack. It was obvious something was annoying you. She naturally assumed her family had outstayed their welcome and you were anxious for them to leave."

"But I was feeling the exact opposite!"

"Unfortunately, your behavior suggested otherwise."

"This is a disaster!" Jack said in a tired voice. "Is there *any* way I can make this right?" He drained the bottle, put it down and covered his face with his hands.

Joseph Harper rose and walked over. Gently squeezing Jack's right shoulder with thin fingers, he said in a strong, calm voice, "Remember, son, the night is always darkest before the dawn."

THE END

Excerpt from *Riding Out the Rough*

Chapter One: High Emotions & Flowing Ink

Macho still had dangerously high testosterone levels after his recent gelding.

Jack had planned to back him today, but the black horse was full of energy this morning and could sense his trainer's weakened state of mind. Instead of allowing the saddle to be placed on his back, the muscular animal was flinging himself around the stall and Jack had to call for assistance.

"Boss, are you sure you want to get on him today?" Luca's voice was wary. The barn manager wasn't in the habit of contradicting his employer. "Wouldn't it be better to lunge him instead?"

Luca's words snapped him out of his idiocy.

Jack's emotions were running as high as the horse's and he almost looked forward to a good battle. It would keep his mind off the bleak thoughts swirling round his brain.

Yet how could he possibly expect to win a full-on fight with an animal as strong-willed as himself but with the added advantage of 800lbs more weight?

More importantly, such behavior ran totally counter to Jack's philosophy. It would undo all the training he'd done so far with Macho – and he'd get hurt in the process. What was the point of that?

He exited the wild horse's stall. "Thanks, Luca, I needed to hear that. Let's put on his lunging gear instead."

Luca was visibly relieved. "We'll get him ready for you, Boss."

Jack nodded to him and to his other rider, Frank.

As he walked past them out of the barn into the sunshine, he caught the two men exchanging confused glances over their boss's troubled state of mind.

Katie, his Golden Retriever, sat with him on the bleachers while he pondered over recent revelations and waited for the pushy horse to be brought to the outdoor arena.

Man, he needed to get a grip on himself!

He'd not slept a wink last night after discovering yesterday that Joe, the teenage client whose bay gelding he had retrained, was his son.

The kid had stayed on the farm during Duke's month-long rehab. As well as conquering the lad's fear of riding his horse, Jack had also helped him overcome his ulcerative colitis and the two had grown very close.

A few weeks later Joe returned for a visit with his adoptive mother, Laura, and Jack had fallen hard for the widow of two years.

It was during an innocent conversation with Laura yesterday, when she and her son were on another trip to his farm, that Jack had suddenly realized exactly who Joe was.

Laura also told Jack that during the adoption process, Joe's birth mother had explained how she'd been bullied by her then boyfriend to get rid of their son, and Laura had made it clear to Jack how much she despised the man.

He could never tell Laura that he was Joe's natural father. How could he admit that *he* was the one who'd told Joe's mother to abort their baby seventeen years ago? If she ever found out Jack was that person, she would never let him see his son – or her – again.

Jack had suggested that the errant father might have repented, but she wouldn't believe it and instead praised the bravery of the mother in keeping the baby, despite being abandoned by Joe's father.

Yet Laura was perfect for him. A caring person with a great sense of humor, she also understood life with a man who has ulcerative colitis. She was a devout Catholic and, having just come back into the Church, Jack appreciated her moral support. And how ideal that she should be the mother of Jack's son!

But his misery over the situation had brought on his taciturn behavior yesterday afternoon and had driven Laura and Joe to cut their visit short.

The emotional stress was taking a toll on Jack's body: bad stomach cramps had kept him up during the night and he knew his ulcerative colitis symptoms were threatening to return.

That same morning, he asked his housekeeper to cut his diet back to the absolute basics.

"Felicia, as soon as Dad leaves, would you mind pureeing my food for the next few days?" This would facilitate digestion and soothe his intestines.

Due to fly back to England that night, Joseph Harper could hardly be asked to eat mashed food on his last day with his son. Jack would simply have to chew his food thoroughly until his father's departure.

"And I hate to ask, but could you make bone broth to add into the mix?"

His Mexican house keeper eyed him with sympathy. She appreciated how the wrong foods and nervous tension could bring on the painful symptoms of constant stomach cramps followed by unexpected diarrhea and bloody stools. He'd had to explain these embarrassing facts when he hired her.

"Si, Señor Jack. I go buy everyting today. Tomorrow you get bone brot and mash food."

Felicia bought beef or pork bones and boiled them in purified water with a dash of apple cider vinegar and one bay leaf for twenty-four hours. They made a nutritious and healing broth that soothed Jack's gut and improved his immune system.

"You're a treasure, Felicia." He gave her a rare hug, glad she didn't ask for explanations.

Mr. Harper senior had not yet appeared for breakfast when Jack left the house to begin his day's training. He wasn't surprised, as they had talked long into the night and his father would be tired. He thought that Robert was probably in the kitchen by now and would soon be out helping with the barn chores. At the request of the boy's parents and Father Michael, his parish priest, Jack was building the bullied kid's self-confidence by having him work on the farm for the rest of the summer.

Normally Robert's mother would drive him to the farm each morning, but the kid was currently staying at the house. His rescue dog, 'Flex, had badly damaged his hind paws after getting stuck in the neighbor's swimming pool two days ago.

Since the boy's father was allergic to pet hair, Jack had agreed to let the dog live at his farm for the time being and for the past two nights Robert had been sleeping on the bedroom floor with his wounded pet. Jack suspected that he wasn't getting the rest he needed, either.

Father Michael had actually adopted the black dog with a white muzzle on his behalf, as part of his mission to evangelize Robert. The teen was more interested in canines than equines and Jack felt that training dogs was good for his self-confidence.

Waiting in the sun for the obstreperous gelding to be led out, Jack thought back on his father's words last night after he'd revealed that Joe was his son – and why he couldn't let Laura know.

Sitting next to Jack on the porch swing, Joseph Harper had rested his bony hand on the younger man's knee. "Son, may I make a suggestion?"

Miserably, Jack mumbled, "Please do!"

"Write her a letter."

Jack looked sideways at his father. "Dad, nothing I write is going to make her feel better about what I did."

"You don't know that." His father's voice was soothing. "Even if she starts out angry at you, she can mull over its contents before she replies."

"How can I be sure she won't rip it up and toss it away?"

"I promise you, she's not going to throw it away. She likes you a lot, son, and wants to believe the best about you. She'll come round."

Jack ran both hands through his disheveled hair. "I wish I shared your optimism, Dad – and I wish I knew what to write that would make her think more favorably about me."

"Just tell her the truth – she'll respect you for that."

Father and son were finally becoming close after decades of being distant towards each other. And now his father was leaving, creating yet another layer of stress which Jack didn't need.

He heard Macho snorting loudly well before Luca and Frank appeared leading the majestic big black horse into the sand arena, one man on either side.

Hormones R Us! He grimaced. *Why did they have to geld him so late?*

He climbed down the bleacher steps and told Katie to lie outside the perimeter fence as he prepared to lunge the feisty steed.

*

Over lunch Jack and his father couldn't bring up last night's conversation since Robert was eating with them.

"How is 'Flex doing?" Joseph Harper asked the boy.

"Not very well, sir, I'm afraid. It's going to take him a long time to get better."

Jack met his father's eyes and the two men grinned. Robert was exaggerating. Why not? It meant he could stay longer on the farm with his beloved dog, rather than go home every night and leave his pet behind.

Jack put a sympathetic expression on his face. "Sorry to hear that, son. We'll hope for the best, though."

"Yes, Mr. Jack."

"We'll also pray for his recovery," Mr. Harper added.

Father and son were aware that Robert was still on the fence regarding his faith in God, despite His having answered their prayers to find the dog when he went missing. Not to mention that it was the priest Father Michael who had dived into the pool to rescue the animal.

Robert replied reluctantly. "Yes, sir."

That afternoon Mr. Harper sat on the bleachers for the last time to watch his son ride his last four client horses. Jack hoped they would soon see each other again: his father had been so comforting last night!

They ate a very early dinner, so Joseph Harper could check into BWI three hours before his 9:50 p.m. flight to London Heathrow. With Robert at the table their conversation continued to be superficial and it wasn't until Jack was driving to the airport that they were able to discuss more burning issues.

En route in the white Evoque Jack admitted that he finally grasped the emptiness his father must be experiencing after the death of his wife of forty plus years.

"I'm not even in a relationship with Laura but I miss her terribly!" Jack said. "It's got to be much worse for you, Dad. I'm sorry I never appreciated that or tried to console you when Mum died."

Mr. Harper's smile was tinged with sadness. "You're doing it now, son." He sat straighter in his seat. "Any more thoughts on writing that letter?"

Jack stared at the road ahead. He'd been thinking about little else, without reaching a decision.

"It's your call," Mr. Harper said, "but at some point, Laura should be told the truth. She should be given the choice of accepting you with your past, or denying her son the opportunity of spending time with his real father." He grinned mischievously. "And of losing the chance of being with the man she is enormously attracted to."

"You're just saying that because you're my father."

"Son, you didn't see how she looked at you when you weren't aware of it, or how confused she became when you insisted the *whole* family come and visit, not just Joe – which you mentioned more than once, as I recall."

Jack grinned. "Yeah, a few times I sensed that she *might* harbor some feelings for me."

"Take it from an old man who's seen a thing or two: she has a lot more than *some* feelings for you."

Jack shrugged his shoulders. "Then why was she so quick to take off yesterday?"

"She's recently lost her husband. She feels vulnerable and is afraid of being mistaken about you and getting hurt again."

"So *that's* why she misread my behavior!"

"Yes, Jack. She wasn't looking for an excuse to leave – she was genuinely worried she'd upset you and beat a retreat before she got hurt any further."

"Oh Dad, what am I going to do without you here to help me understand women?" This was all so bewildering to Jack.

"I'm only a phone call away, son, and you know where I live."

Jack smiled ruefully, thinking of all the years he'd missed with both his parents by running away from them after his stupid mistake with Jill seventeen years ago!

He wanted to cry like a little boy when they reached the airport.

Mr. Harper hugged him. "Good bye, son, I love you and I want you to be happy."

"Bye, Dad, I love you, too."

"Let me know how it goes."

"I will. Wish me luck."

"I'll do better than that – I'll pray hard for you!"

All the way home, feeling lonely and empty, Jack pondered the pros and cons of writing that letter to Laura.

On the plus side, it would allow him to explain his behavior at breakfast yesterday and his efforts to atone for past sins. He could let her know that he was her adopted son's father – or that the likelihood was enormously strong. They could always take a paternity test to make certain that he was right.

But, on the minus side, she would be horrified to learn that it was he who'd insisted his pregnant girlfriend abort their baby. And if Jack turned out *not* to be Joe's son, he would have thrown away all chances of being with Joe and Laura.

Was he willing to take that risk? Was he strong enough to take the consequences of being truthful to her?

Yet could he contemplate a relationship with Laura based on a falsehood by not telling her about his past?

He vacillated back and forth between the two positions the whole way home, and as he swung through the electronic gates onto his drive just after nine o'clock he was still unsure what to do.

Before he even reached the kitchen, he smelled an inviting savory aroma, and once inside he heard the gentle simmering of bone broth in the making. Felicia was being as good as her word.

She was in the sitting room watching a Spanish station on TV and rose as Jack entered. "Buenas noches, señor."

"Good night, Felicia, thank you for making that broth." She smiled with a nod. "And for staying with Robert. I guess he's in bed now?"

She shook her head disapprovingly. "On floor with dog."

Jack laughed. "Good man! See you tomorrow."

"I pray for you, señor." She walked out of the room.

Did he look that sad? He heard her close the front door, and softly called out to Katie. She hadn't greeted him on his return, so he assumed the Retriever was sleeping with Robert and 'Flex.

There was a rustle in boy's bedroom and the Retriever appeared in the hallway. "C'mon, girl, you need a final trip outside." Katie didn't budge. "O.K. I guess you don't. Off you go, traitor."

The dog padded back to Robert's room, leaving Jack feeling even more lonely.

He got ready for bed but there was no point trying to sleep in his present state of mind. His brain told him he'd be an idiot to tell Laura the truth, and then accused him of being a coward because he didn't have the courage to divulge his shameful past to her.

Always touted as the guy who wasn't afraid of taking on any horse, why was he hesitating now?

What harm can it do to just <u>write</u> *the letter? No one's putting a gun to my head and making me send it.*

Wearing his dressing gown and slippers he went into his office and sat down at the large desk. It would be quicker to compose a letter on his laptop and, should he really wish to send it to Laura, he could always copy it out in long hand.

Despite the fact that she may never see what he wrote, his heart was pounding furiously as he turned on the desk lamp. He pressed the 'ON' button of his computer and felt her watching over his shoulder, reading every word.

Dear Laura,

This is painfully hard to write, but I want you to know the truth about me.

You'll remember my telling you there were things I needed to sort out, and you thought I was being deliberately mysterious.

I also told you that I thought I'd done – and had meant to do – something which turns out not to have happened. You complained that I was being even more mysterious.

I can understand why it looked that way to you, but the truth is much simpler. And it makes me look bad.

But our conversation on the way back from Mass on Sunday made certain facts crystal clear to me, and I knew that I would eventually have no choice but to reveal them.

I can see you shaking your head and hear you telling me I'm being mysterious again.

I don't how you feel about me right now, but your opinion of me will be considerably lower by the time you've read what I have to say.

It's not a good story, so I'll keep it short.

Back in England when I was at Bath University, I dated a girl. We both came from strongly Catholic families, so when she became pregnant at the end of our final year, I panicked. Our parents would go crazy!

I was not ready to get married and told her to get an abortion and not tell a soul about it.

In those days I believed that abortion was the only solution and an easy one. I have since come to realize that neither statement is true. Whatever you may think about me, please know that I now understand that abortion is murder.

A job working for a horse trainer became available in the States, so I immediately flew over to take the post. A lot of my motivation to leave England was to put my girlfriend, my parents and what I considered a stupid religion, behind me.

I learned enough from my American employer to leave him and build up my own business and you've seen how happy I am working with horses. They're uncomplicated, unlike us humans, and I understand them better than I do people.

After seventeen years over here, my mother died in England. Away from the Church for so long, I felt alienated at her funeral Mass. I could share more with you about that time, but I doubt you'd be interested.

On my return home I was told a Mr. Brady had called, asking me to take on his nephew, Joe and Joe's horse, Duke. I don't like working with youngsters but when my secretary told me Joe had ulcerative colitis – well, you can appreciate how that changed my mind.

When Joe left after his month with me, I missed him. I'd become fond of him and we have so much in common.

After Joe's departure, Father Michael suggested that I apologize to my ex-girlfriend for what I'd done, and she visited me here in the States just before you brought Joe back here.

In the course of her stay, she said that she didn't have that abortion. She'd given up our son for adoption but had no idea where he was or even if he was still alive. I was thrilled not to have my son's blood on my hands, but at the same time devastated that I would never see him.

Then came your revelations about having adopted Joe in England, how his parents went to Bath University and his father had abandoned the mother to abort the baby.

I think you know by now that I had more than a passing interest in you when you showed up at the farm with Joe. Since then my feelings for you have only grown stronger.

When I realized that Joe was my son, many things fell into place. You'll recall I had difficulty steering and will now understand why.

In the same instant as realizing who Joe was, I also recognized that I had no chance with you. You made it clear that you despised Joe's natural father, and even when I suggested that he might have apologized to his natural mother, you showed skepticism and no inclination to believe such a thing was possible.

I hope you can now look with some compassion on my behavior at breakfast on Sunday? I was struggling with painful new revelations and was not upset with you – I was upset with myself.

Despite what you might believe, I have apologized to Joe's natural mother and understand what a terrible thing I put her through. I am eternally grateful to her for keeping our baby. Our relationship is now that of long-distance friends and I wish her the best.

Joe is much better off with you and having had the benefit of two parents who loved him and each other.

And now that his adoptive father is gone, knowing what you now do, I appreciate that you could never be comfortable *allowing me to have a role in my son's life after what I almost did to him.*

Meeting you has brought me great joy but also great regret, since my past behavior will always be an obstacle for you. You cannot know how badly I wish it were not the case! Take care of Joe for me, Laura. I hold you in my prayers and in my heart.

Yours always,

Jack

He visualized her pulling away from him as he wrote those last words and a deep sadness overtook him.

Back in his room he knelt by his bed asking God to forgive him for his past and to see if, in His Infinite Mercy, He could please give him the courage to send the letter?

Wearily climbing into bed and wondering if he should talk to Father Michael, he became aware of Katie's feet padding softly into the room. She jumped onto the bed and Jack laid his hand on her silky back.

"Thank you, girl," he said and his eyes closed to instant sleep.

About the Author

Now an American citizen, Hilary originally hails from England and lives in Hilton Head, South Carolina with her husband, and two English Bulldogs.

Her writings include Christian inspirational fiction and short stories about horses, other animals and the occasional human. She has also penned a humorous horse memoir, *The Horse Bumbler* series as well as books about competing in dressage and purchasing the ideal horse for a beginner rider.

The rest of her time is spent training and competing on Cruz Bay, the Welsh Cob Thoroughbred Cross she bred and backed, and lamenting the fact that she still has a long way to go before reaching her dressage goals!

However, her real goal is to make it to heaven, and do what she can to encourage others to get there, too.

Acknowledgements

Yet again I was blessed with wonderful beta readers for this second book in the Jack Harper Trilogy, and I want to give them the high praise they deserve.

First of all I wish to express my extreme gratitude to Wendy Emblin, who has devoted countless hours (on and off the phone) and pints of printer ink to editing the first draft of both this and the previous book in the series. Not only have her eagle eyes been invaluable in spotting typos and other errors, but she also has an uncanny instinct for honing on in the sentences I was already uncomfortable with and suggesting/demanding rewrites.

My gentle readers can also thank her for the existence of Tigger, who sprang into life on the pages of the first book because of Wendy's insistence that a barn was not complete without its own feline! I am very glad she did, as he has proved most useful.

I also want to give enormous thanks and credit to the following generous friends for their precious time and input. They are – in alphabetical order: Celeste Behsmann, Marilyn Jackson, Joanne McAlpin, Kelly Rose, Shirley Wilkinson (ladies first!) and Colin Wilkinson.

Thank you also to the following for their help in deciding on the title (again, in alphabetical order):

Wendy Emblin, Celeste Behsmann, Marilyn Jackson, Aviva Nebesky, Kelly Rose, Diannalynn Saufley, Travis Smith, Susie Smyth and Shirley Wilkinson.

I do hope your experience with this novel hasn't put you off beta-reading the final part of this trilogy. My heartfelt appreciation goes out to all of you,

God bless,

Hilary
Rubesca4@gmail.com

Discover Other Books by Hilary Walker

Christian Inspirational

Riding Out the Devil (Book 1 in *The Jack Harper Trilogy*)
Riding Out the Tempest (Book 2 in *The Jack Harper Trilogy*)
Riding Out the Rough (Book 3 in *The Jack Harper Trilogy*)

Riding Out the Turbulence (Companion Short Story to *The Jack Harper Trilogy*)

Riding Out the Wager (Book 1 in *The Father Michael Trilogy*)
Riding Out the Regrets (Book 2 in *The Father Michael Trilogy*)
Riding Out the Wreckage (Book 3 in *The Father Michael Trilogy*)
Brittle Diamonds – a Christian Mystery Novel

Ivan's Choice: A Hilton Head Romance

Saving Prophecy: A Sinclair Island Romance (Book 1)

Equestrian Guides

A Step-By-Step Guide to Entering Your First Dressage Competition

The Beginner Rider's Guide to Stress-Free Horse Buying: *How to Purchase the Perfect Horse for a Beginner Rider without Going Insane*

The Horse Bumbler Series: The Autobiography of an Awful Rider with Aspirations

Part One: First Catch Your Horse
Part Two: You've Caught Your Horse: Now What?
Part Three: The Aim of All This
Part Four: What Horses Do to You

Short Stories

A Perfect Christmas & Other Horse Stories

How I Lost My Husband's Horse

A Dog Named Blue

The Horse Inside

Connect with Me

Visit my website:

https://hilarywalkerbooks.com/

Subscribe to my blogs:

http://christiantales.com/

http://horsetales.weebly.com/

Visit me on Facebook for Upcoming Events:

fb.me/HilaryWalkerBooks

CPSIA information can be obtained
at www.ICGtesting.com
Printed in the USA
BVHW041948020521
606292BV00008B/63